Available in Paperback and Ebook

Cover Design by Tabitha Lennox

Author Blog: https://wordpress.com/home/
thingsiwishidsaid143673148.wordpress.com

WORK, LEISURE AND FORBIDDEN PLEASURE

Joanne Lennox

For Tabitha, for supporting my creative endeavours. I couldn't do it without you.

PROLOGUE

*** Booking: The Lakeside Lodge, 1st - 7th June, for 6 Adults. Paid in full. We look forward to seeing you there!*

*~ Happy Holidays, from the
Lakeside Holiday Park! ***

Would the holiday be happy, though?

Respectable headmaster Joe (48) is at breaking point, wondering how to break it to his wife that he wants a divorce, and desperately searching for some meaning in life. Meanwhile his wife Maggie (also 48) is blissfully unaware that her marriage is about to implode.

Their daughter Lucy (24) seems respectable now, but is keeping a huge, life-changing secret from her partner Barty (45), a secret that dates back to her wilder youth. And Joe and Maggie's son Thomas (22) can't help but feel there is more to life than 9-5 at a soul-destroying job and living from paycheck to paycheck.

And then Maggie's sister Bel (46) has undergone a bitter falling out with her daughter, as she disapproves of her daughter's decision to join the circus and raise her child there. Daughter Sophy (24), a talented acrobat, is hurt by and angry at her mother's rejection of her and her lifestyle. The scene is set for some fireworks that are nothing to do with the circus's closing ceremony...

Life was grey, dreary, money was tight, the rich were OK but most other people were struggling. They needed a holiday.

When the circus rolls into town it brings with it a spirit of forgiveness and romance, casting a strange spell on all those around it...

CHAPTER 1

"Well I don't think it's right," stated Bel, taking a packet of wholewheat pasta from the bag and placing it down on the counter.

"No," agreed her sister Maggie, soothingly, arranging the boxes of herbal tea beside the kettle. You wouldn't know they were sisters to look at them. Maggie was fairly tall, with light brown curls, while Bel was considerably shorter, with hair that was straight and almost black. However, they did have a similar style of clothing, which they would have liked to describe as 'artsy' and 'eclectic'- they bought good quality items relatively cheaply from charity shops, in order to appear to be more middle-class than they actually were. "She was always so good at gymnastics, though, wasn't she?" Maggie continued. "That was why they scouted her."

"It was indeed," Bel agreed. "I blame her father," she added darkly.

"Well," Maggie replied, "*you've* never been that way inclined, have you?"

Bel shook her head. "Not in the least." She paused. "And I mean, bringing up her kid in a circus, for crying out loud!"

"Hmm, yes I suppose it is a rather – unstable environment," Maggie said, as tactfully as she could. "All those – clowns and whatever," she added vaguely.

Bel sighed deeply. "It's selfish, choosing a life as an acrobat, without thinking of that poor child and her education. Always on the move, chopping and changing schools." Bel worked as a teaching assistant at a junior school, while Maggie was an English teacher at a secondary school in the same Hampshire town. Consequently, the sisters were confident that they knew a bit about education, and indeed about most subjects.

Maggie wanted to agree that, yes, it *was* selfish, however, for the moment she remained tactfully silent. She wholeheartedly agreed with her younger sister, but knew it wasn't her place to be too vocal, when it was Bel's daughter who was the butt of the criticism. Such vociferousness could turn around and bite her on the backside at some point in the future.

Presently, however, Maggie saw that Bel had gone quiet and was looking upset, and that something needed to be said. "Still, you must be glad that you'll be seeing Sophy and little Fox this holiday," she ventured. "After all, it's pretty handy, the Circus of Dreams having fetched up just down the road." Indeed, this was partly why Maggie herself had encouraged her husband Joe to book a week's holiday at this particular rural idyll, deep in the Sussex countryside.

"I suppose so," Bel conceded grudgingly, though a

small smile tugged at the corners of her mouth at the prospect. "If Sophy can spare the time to bring the wee one over to visit us. Fox is eight years old now – and I've hardly seen that child since she was born, what with her being at the circus and then things being rather difficult between me and her mother. And I must admit – I miss them, both of them."

"Mmm yes, it would be lovely to see Sophy," Maggie agreed soothingly, "and Fox."

"And what kind of name is that, anyway, Fox?" Bel asked, closing a cupboard door with unnecessary force. She blushed, pre-emptively defensive against anyone who might laugh at her beloved granddaughter's expense. "We'd never have got away with names like that in our day."

"Hmm, I quite like it, though," Maggie said wistfully. "I think it's quite good that you can name your child anything you want these days." She considered all the beautiful names she might have chosen, culled from a selection of the finest literary and artistic references. "And at least," she went on, as tactfully as she could manage, "circus notwithstanding, you *have* a grandchild, Bel." Maggie's brow puckered slightly at the thought that, so far, neither of her own children had managed to provide her with one.

With the food unpacked, the women went and flopped down on the sofa in the sun-dappled sitting-room, sighing with relief. The room was furnished in neutral tones, slightly dull, but tasteful, featuring a long beige sofa adorned with an array of co-ordinating scatter cushions, various neutrals, beige, dark brown, gunmetal grey, balanced in a row on their points. The view through the French doors was stunning; beyond their private fishing veranda could be seen the lake in all its glory in the shimmering sun, surrounded by lush summer greenery and featuring a small central island crowded with an assortment of waterfowl – mallard, mandarin, an Egyptian goose. There was also a spurting jet of water emerging from the dark blue waters, as if Moby Dick himself was down there somewhere. The real explanation was far more prosaic – according to Joe, the fountain was there to keep the lake water moving and also reduce the build-up of algae.

Bel kicked off her navy canvas espadrilles and wriggled her unvarnished toenails. "Kids, eh? Who would have 'em?" she asked, before going on, "I think I made the right decision by only having the one." Although the decision had actually been made for her, by the fact that Sophy's father had buggered off when Sophy was just five years old, and no other suitable suitors had ever turned up for Bel.

"Quite probably," nodded Maggie, who had two. "The problem is, they never really turn out quite how you hoped," she added, gazing reflectively at a circular stone-coloured rug. She and Joe had tried so hard to produce balanced, inquiring children, without the corrupting influence of a TV or social media.

It had seemed to backfire, big-time, in the end. "I mean, take my Thomas. He's a bright enough lad, but he lacks *focus.* So he's got some dead end job picking up rubbish. And then take Lucy." She glanced round furtively before continuing, as if to check that Lucy herself hadn't suddenly turned up. Things were slightly awkward between Maggie and her daughter, a situation which she hoped this holiday would help to repair. "She used to be such a wholesome girl, so focused on her academic career." A version of me is what I mean, Maggie added privately. The 'me' that I would have aspired to be, ideally. She thought back to her daughter's younger years – that slight, mouse-haired figure with the teenage pimples and endearingly dubious fashion sense – a spirited, determined girl, the pocket rocket, Maggie had called her, devoted to her studies. "She was such a clever girl," Maggie sighed. "Loved her English Lit. Well-behaved and polite, too. But then she threw it all away. I was devastated when she left home like that, threw away everything she had! Nowadays for her, it's all about glamour and politics. And fawning over that idiotic partner of hers."

"At least he's rich, though," Bel put in. Barty had inherited wealth, and was the editor of a well-known weekly magazine, that specialised in politics, culture and current affairs – so the story went, Lucy and Barty had met when she got a job as a junior reporter for his magazine. Barty also had ambitions to go into politics. "Good of him to chip in 50 per cent to renting this place for the week," Bel added.

"Yes, it was," Maggie said grudgingly. "We couldn't really have afforded it without him." There were various types of accommodation available at the Lakeside Park, stratified in price bands as strict as the very class system in society: in the case of this Park, it varied at the lowliest level from tents and 'glamping pods', up to Shepherd's huts and through to the pinnacle of luxury, the Lodges, of which they had managed to procure one. "Even so, this probably isn't up to his usual standard of accommodation – I hope he's OK with slumming it for a few days." Maggie looked around her. "Anyway, where the hell's Joe got to? Surely there's only so long you can spend choosing bait?"

"Ah," Bel sighed, "you know what men are like, Mags, he's probably popped off for a quick pint at the club house."

Maggie's expression darkened. "I hope not, I don't want him to get a beer belly! I mean, if he's expecting me to give him his conjugal rights, is it too much to ask that he keeps himself reasonably attractive? Not that the conjugal rights have been happening much lately." The two women cackled together. "Women always seem to love him, though," Maggie went on thoughtfully. "A fact that he's fortunately unaware of. And personally, I can't see it any more, myself. Perhaps, if you spend too many years looking at someone's face across the breakfast table, you simply get bored of it…"

"Hmm, most likely," Bel agreed.

"Is there anything decent on to watch?" Maggie went on, suddenly tired of the subject. "Pass me that TV guide, Bel."

*

As he drank his beer at the club house, Joe thought about his life. All in all, it was a pretty sorry state of affairs. He hated his job – he found teaching a totally thankless task these days. He was heartily sick of league tables, inspections, stats gathering. As for the pupils, most of them were fine, but the behaviour of the minority was appalling. He was regularly sworn at, occasionally assaulted. His working days were long, ten to twelve hours - as a head teacher, there was no limit to the hours he was expected to work, and then there was the commute. Then at the weekend there were chores to do, social visits to pay. And when he finally *did* have any time to himself, he was too exhausted to do anything.

Joe gazed unseeingly through the window of the clubhouse, and thought about the other big problem in his life - his marriage. Things between him and Maggie seemed to have broken down completely. Their physical attraction had diminished over the years, ebbing away like water down a plughole, and mentally they just seemed to bore eachother now. She scoffed at the things he liked, such as fantasy role playing games, historical military stuff and so on. And he wasn't too keen on the things *she* liked doing, like going up to London to see a musical; or to the theatre to see some overly-earnest, pretentious play, or for dinner at an over-priced restaurants where the portions were tiny.

Playing Dungeons and Dragons was one of the few things that still made Joe happy - not least because of the escapism it brought. For decades now, he and his old schoolmates had got together every few months for a session, gathering round someone's table and exploring a fantasy world together, while pretending to be a dwarf or an elf, a fighter or a wizard. It was great, they could lose themselves in their roles and forget about everyday life. But his mate John, who organised it, had had a major operation a few weeks ago, and hadn't replied to Joe's most recent email. Feeling a twinge of anxiety now, Joe tugged at the uncomfortable red neckerchief that Maggie had made him wear. God, it was hot.

He sighed. It seemed to him as though any pleasure he ever felt in life was just relief - although maybe all pleasure was relief. Human beings were born without their own consent, and if they were lucky they died without their own consent. And they were complicit in an economic system that was basically just a - a blood engine. He glanced across to the seating area outside the bar, and saw a happy family eating ice-creams. Now *there* was something - ice-cream was great, sure, but then if you thought about how other people had to suffer to produce it - the factory workers, the lorry drivers, the poor cows that produced the milk. OK, maybe he was overthinking things. But that was the trouble with being a teacher. You picked up a lot of knowledge you would rather not know. And then you were duty-bound to tell the pupils. No wonder more and more young people were turning to veganism these days...

Joe sipped at his beer. Everything just seemed horrific. The economic system was grown from the environment it was created on – life feeding on life, even the ground you walked on was decay: maggots, worms and shit. It was just corpses all the way to the ground. He'd had enough of it. He dreamed of chucking in his job, leaving his wife and doing something new before it was too late. He had a crazy dream that they could split the value of their house and he could buy a run-down cottage somewhere cheap, the wilds of Wales maybe, and live off-grid. He'd been to Wales once for a holiday, as a child, somewhere in the north. A beautiful, magical place; he particularly remembered clambering about in a steep rocky valley, lush with vegetation.

It wouldn't take much to make Joe happy, just a simple life. A life without all the clutter, all the *stuff*. He'd tried to talk to Maggie about how unhappy he was, but she'd batted his attempts away, as if the idea was an annoying fly. The thing was, Maggie still loved her job as a teacher.

"My favourite time is when the new students start at the school," she'd said the other day over breakfast, in a voice that glowed with enthusiasm, "and you're faced with a classful of pupils with shining eyes and upturned faces, pure empty vessels just waiting to be filled with knowledge!"

"O-*kay*," Joe had said – he could see where she was coming from though he thought her imagery a little fanciful.

"And of course," she went on eagerly, "It's *really* rewarding when a kid from a poor background gets a place at Oxbridge, isn't it?"

"Well yes, of *course* it is," Joe replied, nodding earnestly, "but those occasions are as rare as hen's teeth, Mags!"

Maggie bridled. "That's as may be," she shot back. "But for that one girl - Jane Smith or whoever - it means the world!"

She was absolutely right. Maggie's feelings were commendable. And Joe was happy for her - of *course* he was - that she still liked her work. But the fact that she seemed fine with their current existence made him feel like he was taking crazy pills. God, the whole thing sucked so much. Sometimes he felt like he hated being alive.

Sighing bitterly now, he drained his pint glass. Of course, alcohol was one form of escape from his life, but he knew it wasn't the answer. Joe picked up his tub of bait, and began to trudge reluctantly back to the lodge. The precious half-term holidays, his week off, was being spent here when he'd rather be at home. And that was another thing, renting this place was costing an arm and a leg. All those hours of misery at work, squandered on something like this, a crappy wooden house in the middle of nowhere, money for old rope.

The path back to the lodge took him closer to the lake. Joe eyed the water uneasily – despite the fact that he could swim, he had a bit of a fear of water, especially dark water like this, where you couldn't see the bottom. Just looking at it now made his heart-rate speed up. The mud, the tangling weeds could pull you down, he felt. But he knew it was something he would have to overcome if he was to live in the wild. Of course, Maggie had been wild swimming a couple of times with friends, and loved it…

Suddenly the loud hooting of a car horn from nearby made him jump. Looking round, he saw Barty at the wheel of a large car on the track beside him, grinning and waving. Barty was a bit of an oaf, but he was fun. And there beside him was Joe's daughter Lucy. Joe always loved to see his children. For the first time in several days, he felt his heart lift.

*

Maggie and Bel were glancing over the *Radio Times,* conferring about televisual matters; they were avid telly watches, and these discussions were one of their favourite pastimes. Maggie was particularly obsessed, as she and Joe had never owned a TV until six or seven years ago, around the time Lucy had left home. They'd believed that by banning the

TV they would create the best possible environment for raising their two children. But once she'd finally caved in, Maggie began to make up for lost time. Her discussion with Bel now was rapid and heated, conducted in a kind of shorthand: *I tried watching that. It's shit. No, he can't act – he can only do comedy. Have you watched this one? I thought it was rubbish. Yes it was, wasn't it? I don't really watch much TV.* Pause for Bel to gaze at Maggie in flabberghasted disbelief. *Live, I mean! It's all on-demand, that's what I meant. Oh, I see.* 'The Winter of the Heir' *is good. What side's that on? BBC 1. Ooh. I haven't seen that before, I'll have to give it a go....*

The two women greatly enjoyed their critiquing, their gentle bitching sessions. Presently they were interrupted by the sound of a car's tyres scrunching on the gravel outside. Car doors were slammed with a satisfyingly heavy clunk and lively voices could be heard through the open kitchen window. The two sisters turned to gaze at eachother, heads cocked, faces puckered with the effort of trying to ascertain who was approaching, seconds before three people strode up the steps and in through the door of the lodge, first in line being Maggie's husband Joe, a tall man of medium build, with a handsome, high-cheekboned face, swept back salt-and-pepper hair, a beard, and horn-rimmed glasses. He would have cut a dashing figure; however, he was currently dressed in beige knee length shorts and a blue checked shirt, accessorised with a red Paisley neckerchief, and bowed under the weight of two heavy suitcases. Clothes-wise, the entire outfit was chosen by Maggie, as Joe really couldn't be bothered these days. She had made him wear the neckerchief 'to add a splash of colour'. Despite Maggie's efforts with the neckerchief, Joe looked exactly what he was, a head teacher off-duty. However, Joe was looking happier than he had done in days, as he led his daughter, plus Richard Bartholomew, (or 'Barty' as he was known), through the doorway of the lodge.

"Joe's a total nerd," Maggie sometimes said (rather spitefully) to her sister, when she was feeling particularly irritated with him. "Of course he's a nice enough man, but he can be so bloody boring. Droning on about his pet subjects. Dungeons and Dragons. War strategy. History. He drives me up the wall sometimes." However she would never have considered divorce as an option, and clung tenaciously on to their marriage.

Joe was currently listening raptly to the aforementioned Barty, a stocky man in his mid forties, clad in cargo shorts and an extremely loud red Hawaiian shirt which clashed with his messy red hair. Barty was showing off the brand new watch that adorned his wrist. "It's a Patek Philippe," he was saying proudly. "70,000 quid that set me back. Still, I like to think of it as more of an investment."

Joe gazed at the watch, which appeared innocuous enough with its tan leather strap and pale golden face. Normally Joe would have thought it a ridiculous waste to spend more than ten pounds on a watch. However, he seemed to have a strange fascination with Barty, who in his eyes could do no wrong. "It looks fantastic," Joe nodded sagely. "They do say that you get what you pay for."

Behind the two men came Lucy, a petite, slender young woman with golden hair swept up in a neat chignon, teamed with a smart pink suit teamed with a silky white blouse. Her fingernails were glossy, neat and pistachio green, having been recently manicured. It was as if she was dressed for a day at the office or maybe the races, rather than a holiday.

Joe dumped the heavy suitcases he was carrying on the floor, and flexed his fingers gratefully.

"Maggie!" Barty approached her, beaming in greeting and bonhomie, stretching out a large hand for her to shake. "And, er – er –"

"Bel," Bel supplied simperingly. Observing her sister, Maggie raised an eyebrow. Any more deferential, she thought, and Bel would be tugging her forelock. Bel seemed to be more easily intimidated than *she* was by the likes of Barty. The two sisters had come from a lower-middle class family; they'd both gone to a good state school and were pretty well-educated. However in subsequent years, borne along on the tide of life, one had gone slightly up in the world, while one had gone slightly down. If you wanted to mix your metaphors, you could say, like a see-saw that had started from rest.

"- Bel!" Barty boomed now in his plummy voice. "Great to see you both again!" He pumped both of their hands, one after the other, causing their bodies to pull and twitch as if they were puppets.

Now it was Lucy's turn to step forward, and she smiled hesitantly at her mother, but did not speak.

"Hello, darling," Maggie smiled encouragingly back. She had felt the customary surge of love mingled with guilt at the sight of her daughter. She was aware that she'd been pretty strict (too strict?) with the children when they were growing up - Maggie did feel bad about that now. I mean, she thought, that had to be why Lucy had rebelled so dramatically, aged seventeen. Ah well, hopefully this holiday would be the perfect opportunity for her to build bridges, and maybe even apologise...

"Hello, Mummy," Lucy said, coming over and kissing the air near Maggie's cheeks. A cloud of expensive perfume surrounded the younger woman, and she smelt as fragrant and flowery as a summer meadow.

Maggie's guilt dissipated, to be replaced with mild irritation. Gazing at Lucy, she could not help wondering when she had started doing that pretentious air-kissing business. And calling her 'mummy'? When, ever since the age of five, she had been content to call her plain old 'Mum'. More to the point, how and when had Lucy picked up that upper-middle class inflection to her voice - was it just through spending so much time with Barty? Or had she made a deliberate effort to acquire it, like learning a script?

"Where's the little boys' room? I need to siphon the old python," Barty said, thundering off down the length of the lodge without waiting for an answer. Lucy shuddered slightly at the crassness of her partner's language. Barty didn't always get things right, but deep down she loved him and wanted to educate him. She felt he was worth the effort. After all, he'd been there for her when she'd really needed someone.

Lucy perched elegantly on the beige sofa, from which she gazed out at the wonderful view of the lake. "This place looks nice; the decor in here is very beige though. The campsite was bloody hard to get to, too!" If Barty had been present, she would have substituted 'bloody' for 'jolly'. But Barty was still in the bathroom so she could cut loose. She felt hot and exhausted; the clip for her chignon was digging into her scalp, and it was all she could do not to flop down carelessly into the cushions. She did not want to appear like a slob, however. "Trust you guys to have chosen this place in the back of beyond."

Joe sighed heavily. "It may be remote, but sadly, even here there's no escape from the slippery tentacles of Boundstone Comprehensive." He fetched a sheaf of papers and sat down heavily on the other end of the sofa. "If I don't get this coursework marked I'm going to be up shit creek when term starts again next week."

"Well maybe if you get the work done nice and quickly, Dad, then you can relax and enjoy the holiday," Lucy suggested brightly.

"Well perhaps," Joe sighed again. "But I don't hold out much hope."

Bel scanned the room around her, as if taking stock. "Hmm, are we all here?" she asked. "Who are we missing?"

"Why, Thomas, of course!" Lucy said, referring to her beloved brother. Thomas still lived at home, but whereas his parents had travelled down the previous day, he'd had to work.

"Oh yes," Maggie agreed. "I *knew* there was someone! How could we forget darling Thomas?"

CHAPTER 2

Thomas was travelling by train. The train had been slightly delayed by staff shortages, but now here he was, well on his way. A tall young man with floppy blond hair, he sat with his size 13 feet propped up on the seat opposite, and his big rucksack on the seat beside him. Cars were bad for the environment, and he couldn't afford one anyway. (As it was, the train fare was costing him an arm and a leg.) Presently his train drew up at a tiny station, more of a halt than a real station. At first Thomas thought they must have stopped there by mistake, but it turned out that it was *him* who'd made the mistake. People often said he was a little scatty. As he gazed out of the window he saw the countryside baking in the hot summer's day with perfect stillness all around; there were willow trees, willow herb, faded grass; everything around was as still as the small clouds high in the sky. It was almost eerie, Thomas thought; there was no sign whatsoever of any people on the platform. It reminded him of *Adelstrop*, a poem they'd done at junior school as one of the teachers liked it. That poem was quite true to life, really, he mused, thinking back. You want to prolong the moment but you can't. Time always moves on. That's what he'd taken it to mean at the time, anyway.

Suddenly Thomas realised it *was* his station and leapt out. He was the only one who got off, and after the train door had slammed behind him the only sound was birdsong. He heard ... blackbirds, chiff chaffs, robins... Frowning, Thomas consulted Google maps on his phone, then trekked off down the country lanes with his rucksack on his back, looking out for more birds and wildlife on his way.

*

Sitting on the sofa, Lucy flexed her dainty feet. It was such a relief to be out of the car. It had taken them ages to get there from London, following the sat nav, Barty taking the bends too fast in his big BMW, as they zoomed down infinite leafy green, narrow roads, turning corners in an endless labyrinth till it seemed you couldn't possibly get any deeper into the Sussex countryside.

When they finally did arrive, it was almost as if they had landed up in some sort of alternative reality. You would never have thought they were only a few miles from the town of Haughton. The place looked like it existed in a kind of time-warp.

Lucy, her parents and aunt sat around now on the sofa and armchairs. The women looked at their phones, while Joe shuffled listlessly through his school paperwork. Having bagsed the master bedroom for himself and Lucy, Barty had gone for a lie-down. Taking surreptitious glances at them, Lucy felt the old resentment bubbling up against her parents, for how they had ruined her childhood, not allowing her and Thomas the freedom that other youngsters had. Not even allowing them a TV! Lucy sighed. She missed her brother. If only he would hurry up and arrive.

Right on cue, a voice from the doorway called, "Hi, folks!", and in trudged Thomas, laden down beneath his heavy rucksack. Everyone descended on him, offering greetings and hugs. He took off his rucksack, and then Lucy took him eagerly by the hand.

"Come and sit down, Thomas, you must be knackered. Ah well, everyone's here now," Lucy added happily. "The holiday can really begin."

"I'll put the kettle on," Bel said, retreating to the well-appointed kitchen. She was feeling rather envious and outnumbered by Maggie's side of the family, and felt a secret hankering, though she knew she mustn't, for the sake of her dignity, to pop over to the circus in the next village and pay a visit to her daughter and granddaughter. Bel had brought with her, on the holiday, a little gift for Fox, just in case they should meet up. It was a copy of the Jacqueline Wilson novel *Lily Alone,* which Bel had come across through her work as a teaching assistant, and thought was a very good, imaginative book. She hoped against hope that at some point during the coming week, she would have the opportunity to give it to her little granddaughter.

*

Later, as evening descended over the lake, and the ducks went home to roost, they all ate pesto pasta and garlic bread cooked by Maggie. "Delicious," everyone agreed. "Thanks, Maggie." Barely had the last mouthful been swallowed, than Lucy and Thomas announced their intention of going to the circus.

"What, *tonight?*" Maggie asked.

"Yes. How about it?" Thomas suggested to the assembled group. "A fun family trip, a great bonding experience, who wants to come?"

There was a brief silence, during which Lucy imagined a tumbleweed rolling past. "It'll be a great opportunity to see Sophy and Fox," she added coaxingly. "D'you want to join us, Aunty Bel?"

Bel felt suddenly flustered, as the prospect of seeing her daughter and granddaughter became an imminent reality. Suddenly she felt guilty that she'd been badmouthing Sophy to Maggie, and almost felt she wouldn't be able to look her daughter in the eye if they did meet face to face. "Oh gosh, no," she stuttered. "Thanks but it's not really my kind of thing, the circus." She began to pile the plates up on top of eachother, almost dropping one through nerves. "Maybe they can come over here another time, and we can all have a nice cup of tea together instead!"

"But why would you *not* want to come, Aunt Bel?" Thomas asked in bafflement. "Surely you want to see them? And besides, circuses are fun!" Sometimes Thomas could be quite single-minded, and could not understand why someone might have an opinion different from his own.

"Thomas!" Maggie hissed at her son. "Leave your aunty alone. If she doesn't feel ready, then that's her business. Look, she's getting upset!"

They all turned to look at Bel, which was probably the last thing she wanted. Her lip was trembling, and she was wiping a stray tear from her eye.

"OK, if you're sure," said Thomas. "But *I* think circuses are fun." He looked around the room. "Who's up for it?" No-one stirred. "Come on you miserable lot, let's not just sit around, where's your spirit of adventure?"

"I'm pretty whacked to be honest," Barty said. "Besides which, I really need to get on with writing *'John Donne and the Metaphysical Poets'*. The publisher is threatening to ask for the advance back if I don't deliver something soon."

"And let me guess," Lucy said, raising an eyebrow. "You've already spent it."

Barty looked sheepish. "Well, not to put too fine a point on it – yes."

"Oh, *Barty!*" Lucy exclaimed. "You're not only a procrastinator, but you're a bore, for not wanting to go on any fun outings!"

Barty went pink with indignance. "Now come on, Muffin, that's hardly fair –"

"Mum?" Thomas prompted.

"No thank you," Maggie said. "I just want to stay in and rewatch *Killing Eve*."

"Boring, boring!" Thomas exclaimed. "You're bloody boring, the lot of you. What about you, Dad?" he asked, turning to his father in desperation.

"I don't know," Joe said gloomily. "Doesn't it seem rather sad, outdated, now? Aren't circuses pretty pointless without the animals?" He paused, a faraway expression entering his eyes. "When I was a kid, there used to be lions and black panthers, you could go and look at them in their cages afterwards, barely believable now! Yes, I *know* it was cruel," he added, seeing that his wife and children were looking daggers at him, "and it's good it's been banned nowadays, but I don't really see the entertainment in watching a load of grown adults prancing around in the big top wearing silly dressing-up clothes." This was quite a long speech for Joe, but it came from the heart. Years ago Joe and Maggie had taken Lucy and Thomas to a circus of this ilk. It hadn't been at all Joe's kind of thing, all that showiness and glitz. He'd much rather have been playing D'n'D of course, which, like a circus, was an escape from reality, and had the added advantages of a more intimate setting, that you were surrounded entirely by friends, and you could actually participate yourself. "And I expect the tickets are pretty pricy too, aren't they?" Joe added.

"Twenty to forty quid, depending on what seats you want," Thomas said. "You old skinflint," he added, making Lucy giggle.

"Well there you go then," Joe said, thinking of how many hours or minutes of misery at Boundstone Comprehensive it would have taken him to earn sufficient money to pay for circus tickets all round. He tended to think of everything in these terms, nowadays.

"Good God!" Thomas exclaimed. "No wonder our childhoods were so boring!"

"Your father has a point, though, Thomas, my lad," Barty piped up. "Circuses are ridiculous things. Where's the culture? It's hardly Shakespeare, is it? Hardly a Tchaikovsky ballet. It's just crude exhibitionism. And a load of sweaty people sitting in a tent watching it. Utterly pointless."

"But the performers are highly skilled –" Lucy began, but her mother interrupted her.

"What about your aunty's feelings, children? It would be very awkward for her if you were to go. It's a very sensitive situation."

Yes, Lucy thought, the resentment boiling up again, it's only sensitive because Aunty Bel has made it that way, by behaving like a bitch towards Sophy.

"It's fine," Bel insisted tearfully. "Let them go."

"And how are you two kids going to get there?" Maggie went on. "It's right out in the sticks, and neither of you can drive."

Lucy looked defiant. "We'll get an Uber, of course, if no-one'll give us a lift. Barty?" she prompted.

Barty looked flustered. "Sorry, Muffin, but I really ought to get straight down to my writing." Secretly he had plans to open up a nice bottle of barolo whilst he prepared to put pen to paper – or rather, finger to keyboard. He smiled at this pleasing inner vision. He'd already set himself up a cushy mini-office in the master bedroom that he and Lucy were sharing. He couldn't wait to start using it.

"Jeez, thanks a bunch!" Lucy exclaimed. "Thanks for nothing, everyone!" and she turned on her heel and flounced out of the lodge. Thomas paused to give everyone a reproachful glare, then stomped off after her.

As soon as they had gone, Maggie could have kicked herself. So much for her plans to build bridges between herself and Lucy! And now she had pissed off the ever-amenable Thomas, too. She was unsure why she had just behaved as she had, doing everything she could to stop the pair of them from doing something as innocent as going to the circus. Most likely, she realised, it all came down to Control. Maggie had always wanted to be in control of her life; it made her feel safe, secure; and yet it seemed as if the older she got, the more everything was slipping out of her grasp. First Lucy leaving home, followed by Thomas's struggles to get a decent job, and then Joe acting so discontented lately... Maggie sighed. It struck her that drastic action might be needed, if she was to repair her relationship with her children. She sensed she was going to have to 'chill out' a bit, and somehow learn to 'go with the flow'. As an English teacher, she didn't really approve of the excessive use of idioms, but sometimes they just seemed to succinctly sum up exactly how you felt.

*

As their Uber zoomed off into the distance, Lucy and Thomas wandered into the meadow, following the signs that read, *'To the Circus of Dreams'*. "How exciting, can't believe no-one wanted to join us for this," Thomas said scornfully to his sister. "Sod them, sod the lot of them!"

"I know, it's just a bit of a hoot, isn't it? Something different," Lucy agreed as they walked across the field. It was a relief to have escaped from the lodge, and the bad atmosphere that had built up there. "I didn't know it would cause such a big argument. Although I should have known - our parents always were the Fun Police. Anyway, it's their loss; it's nice to get away from them, and be just the two of us."

Thomas winked at her. "Partners in crime, eh, just like the old days." The two – who, as toddlers had been hyperactive and mischievous - had been quite a handful together back in the day. Before they had been old enough to go to school. That was before Maggie and Joe had really clamped down on them.

"Exactly. And I'm so looking forward to seeing Sophy and Fox," Lucy added with a smile of anticipation. Because of the family circumstances, they didn't get to see them nearly enough.

The Big Top loomed up before them, an enormous tent nestling in the flowery meadow. Its roof was red and yellow striped, reaching up to a peak like a mountain top, with a flag proudly stuck aloft. Lucy and Thomas bought their tickets at a nearby kiosk and went inside.

No sooner had they passed through the doorway than the atmosphere settled upon them. It was dark, bustling, magical, the very air seemed to twitter with anticipation. It felt completely different from circuses they had been to before. For starters, no-one was in their seats yet. People were wandering around, gazing up at the massive heights of the big top. It was like a vast black night sky, lit with twinkling rainbow coloured lights. And the circus performers were milling around amongst the audience, stopping to chat to people as they went. There was a woman in a straw boater with yellow streamers attached, waving a huge blue and red flag, a man in a red satin military-style jacket playing the accordion, a man holding a huge bunch of multicoloured balloons while riding a unicycle, a woman swinging round a pole, fully dressed in a kind of peasant costume, skirts flaring out.

"Ladies and gentlemen," announced a voice over the loudspeaker.

At that moment Thomas spotted a glamorous red-headed figure in the crowd of performers, clad in a spangled outfit that showed an awful lot of leg. It was his cousin. "There's Sophy! *Sophy!*" he called.

But Sophy was walking away, being absorbed by the crowd, her red hair streaming out behind her, waving, calling, mouthing, "Sorry! Got to go!" The audience were hurrying to their seats, as if this was all one massive game of 'musical chairs'.

Sure enough, no sooner had Thomas and Lucy got into their seats than the show exploded into life. There was a glamorous woman spinning a hoop on every limb, muscular acrobats somersaulting, landing on the shoulders of other performers, a woman dangling, spinning from her dark rope of hair, up and down. Motor cyclists inside a large metal mesh ball, crossing and re-crossing eachother's paths. Someone spinning plates on sticks. But Sophy the Trapeze artist was the star of the show, a gorgeous, curvaceous flame-haired figure in a tight-fitting outfit the colour of sapphires and amethysts, high up in the spotlight, making Lucy feel dowdy by comparison, a feeling she had not experienced since her teenage years of baggy jeans, grungy cardigans and a monobrow. Sophy swung from the trapeze; flung herself away from it, leapt through the air, catching back onto it with her strong legs. Thomas watched, worried and excited. Sophy's red-lipsticked mouth beamed. She was a born performer; she revelled in the attention. Even Fox had a turn, dancing on a little stage, twirling some hoops. She was a good mover, another natural.

"Well, that was magic, wasn't it?" Lucy said afterwards. Thomas nodded his agreement. It really had been great; for the hour or two it had lasted, it seemed to have taken them completely out of everyday life.

The two of them wandered off to find Sophy. The Ring Mistress, a large, imposing lady with a mass of frizzy dark hair, a sparkly black bodysuit and fishnet tights and high-heeled red shoes, directed them to the little red and white caravan at the corner of the field, where Sophy lived with Fox. "We really enjoyed the show," Lucy told the Ring Mistress smilingly. "It was fantastic."

"Why, thank you so much," the Ring Mistress replied. She gestured around the meadow they were crossing, at the happy crowds departing, children chattering away, carrying balloons and glow sticks. "That's what it's all about, for me, bringing a little joy and colour into people's lives. People need it; they can't get by without it."

In the caravan, they were introduced to Fox, a pretty girl, dark-haired and with odd-coloured eyes, one brown and one blue. Fox was already in her pink, fluffy pyjamas, and was just off to bed. Once the little girl was safely tucked up in the tiny bedroom, Sophy sat Lucy and Thomas down at her little table and offered them lemonade. It was only economy lemonade from the supermarket, but somehow it was extra delicious. Perhaps Sophy's presence was some kind of enchantment, Lucy wondered. Even close up, she was beautiful in an otherworldly way, kind of elfin, with her long red hair, pointy cheekbones and green eyes. She had showered and changed into a black top, and green trousers, which accentuated her tiny waist and hourglass figure. "I always want to get out of my fishnets as soon as possible," she explained. "Otherwise they leave a horrible deep mark ingrained in your skin. So," she added, "What did you guys think of the show?"

"We thought you were fantastic!" Thomas said, his eyes wide with enthusiasm.

"You're so talented," Lucy added.

Sophy shrugged, her eyes downcast. "My mum thinks I'm selfish for doing what I do."

"Huh! What a bitch," said Lucy, enjoying the freedom to speak as she found. She might have softened her language a bit if Barty had been present. And she would certainly not have been so blunt to Aunty Bel's face.

"No, I've been thinking, maybe I *am* selfish," Sophy said, looking guilty. "When I first thought about joining the circus I wasn't sure, because I knew I'd be taking Fox out of ordinary life. But then I convinced myself it'd be OK." Suddenly her green eyes brimmed over and she burst into tears. "The thing is, I'm getting to the point now where I'm not sure I can do this any more," she sobbed, wiping her eyes with the back of her hand.

"What, you don't want to be a trapeze artist any more?" Thomas asked. "But you're so good! It would be a crime to give it up!"

Sophy shook her head. "No, it's not that I don't want to be an aerialist any more – I love the trapeze – it's part of me! But it's Fox. It's not fair on her. Moving around, going to a different school every few weeks. Apparently Fox has dyscalculia, poor love, and she really struggles with numbers and stuff. And then, as if this wasn't enough, each school she goes to is doing a different part of the syllabus, so I've been trying to do a bit of home schooling to make up the gaps. But it's too much, I can't go on like this. I've been thinking I'll have to give it up, and get a regular job in an office or something."

"Oh Soph, it's terrible you've been feeling so desperate!" Lucy exclaimed, reaching her hand across the table. Besides the long mint-green nails, there was a flower tattoo on Lucy's inner wrist that she'd had done before she met Barty (she often tried to keep the tattoo hidden as Barty didn't really approve of them). She was going to rub Sophy's hand comfortingly but then thought better of it, and instead came round the table to envelope her cousin in a full-blown hug. "Come here, sweetie." After a minute or so she released Sophy, who was looking a bit crumpled but slightly happier.

"Now listen to me," Lucy said firmly. "You, as a woman, are perfectly entitled to work at your chosen career, while also being a mum. If you were a man, there would be no question about it. You agree, Thomas?" Solemnly he nodded his agreement.

"But what am I going to do?" Sophy asked in

despair.

Lucy thought for a moment. "Well, for starters we could just give you a bit of a break, and see how the land lies after that. I know it's half-term at the moment but you could probably still use a break. We're staying at the lakeside lodge just down the road for a week, how about Fox comes to stay with us while we're there? If she brought her school books with her, I'm sure someone could do a bit of extra learning with her if you wanted."

Sophy gasped. "I couldn't do that. Of course I'd miss Fox, but anyway, I couldn't lumber you guys with her, not while you're on your vacation. I mean, lumber is the wrong word. She is adorable."

"She *is* adorable. And it wouldn't put us out at all," Lucy said firmly. "It would be a pleasure to have her."

"Yeah, it would be cool," Thomas agreed. "And it would be a great chance for Fox to get to know her granny."

"You guys are so kind," Sophy said, drying her tears on a fresh tissue provided by Lucy. "And Fox is a good kid. Easy-going and pretty great with adults, for an eight year old – I mean, she's around them all the time, so she's bound to be." Sophy was already looking happier; lighter, somehow. "Hopefully she won't be too much trouble for you."

*

Lucy was awakened at eight the next morning

by the sunlight pouring in through the thin floral curtains. She went and had a quick shower, and then returned to the bedroom, where Barty still lay snoring in the bed, to do her make-up. Moving quietly so as not to wake him, she set up her own cosmetics mirror on the windowsill, the mirror she took everywhere, 15X magnification. Even after all this time, she still felt a bit uncomfortable about Barty seeing her without her make-up on. Every morning she painted her face like an English rose, as she had decided this was what she wanted to be. Concealer, foundation, a gentle pink blush, drifting across the uplands of her cheeks. Lucy was a firm believer in improving on what mother nature had given you, though it hadn't been until her period of teenage rebellion that she had realised this. (Her skin had improved as she got older anyway, and even if she had an occasional break-out due to stress or the time of the month, she was expert at applying make-up to disguise it.) It had been one of the big revelations of her life when, aged seventeen, she had 'acquired' a blemish concealer (stolen it in fact, but that was another story). Before that, her spots had convinced her she was ugly, and that that was why her mother had encouraged her to focus on an academic career. However, the discovery of that flesh-coloured, lipstick style cosmetic had transformed Lucy's life. She realised with the use of concealer she could look quite pretty - her actual features were fine, not ugly at all. At that moment she discovered the delights of Control. And realised that everything could be hers for the taking.

When she'd reached breaking point, Lucy had rebelled against her stifling upbringing, and swapped principles for pragmatism, academia for ambition. This took her on a path of recklessness and risk-taking, until finally she had met Barty; he took a liking to her, and she'd got a job as a journalist on his magazine, *The Witness.* Their relationship had developed and she'd moved into his luxury London apartment. The only fly in the ointment had come when, after a few years together, Barty had suggested they start trying for a baby. He already had one adult son but was keen to add to his brood. This made Lucy anxious and uneasy - and the reason was that she knew that she was infertile, due to something that had happened during that period of recklessness when she was eighteen.

The simplest solution would have been to come clean to him about this. However she was terrified that if Barty found out she couldn't have children, he would dump her. And so she'd kept it from him. They had been trying for months now; she wished she could have carried his baby; she wanted to make him happy, because she loved him. Sure, Barty's moods could be difficult but he was, on the whole, kind, he seemed genuinely fond of her, and they had a lot in common, such as their shared love of books and interest in all things cultural. Looks-wise, other people didn't see what she saw in him, but she quite liked his bulk, it made her feel dainty. And his noble face with its roman nose. Physically, things were good between them, there was an easygoing, natural chemistry. In fact, they had made love last night, after she'd returned from the circus all full of magic (*everyone* in the lodge had been all a-flutter, once they arrived back with little Fox in tow, especially Bel, who had burst into delighted tears at the sight of her granddaughter. The bad atmosphere that had existed before the circus had completely vanished), and Barty had been mellow and liberated by the bottle of Barolo he had consumed. No doubt he was hoping even now that he might finally have got her pregnant, though Lucy knew the odds of that happening were slim.

Oh, if only the miracle could happen! A baby would be another silken bond that would tie him to her - which seemed necessary to assuage her insecurity as they were not yet married or even engaged. Having a baby together would cement their relationship, and would doubtless lead to him proposing to her. The worst case scenario - the one Lucy feared - was that his attention would drift to someone else who *could* give him a child, as she knew he had a short attention span and his eyes were likely to wander. She would be devastated if he left her, and her life would be in disarray.

Barty had had no shortage of relationships, indeed, he had been married twice before, a fact that she largely tried to ignore, and she had deliberately never asked to see any photos either of his previous wives or of the twenty-three year old son that he had from his first marriage. She didn't think her fragile confidence could take it. So far he'd never invited her to go along when he met up with his son, Sebastian, and she had never asked if she could go.

An hour or so later, as everyone was sitting on the sunny balcony having breakfast, Barty leant back in his chair and said, "It's jolly nice here. I might see if my son and his ladyfriend want to come down and visit for a few days."

Spreading her piece of bread with marmalade, Lucy bristled with trepidation.

"Oh that's nice," Maggie said. "Will they be able to get the time off work?"

"Well they're environmental activists, and they're a bit in the doldrums at the moment, as they've just been evicted from the Lambeth Tunnel. They've been protesting against that new rail link – Sebastian and I don't exactly see eye to eye on political matters," he chuckled, "but blood's thicker than water as they say."

Lucy sat up a little straighter. Barty had never mentioned his son being an environmental activist before. Perhaps he was embarrassed of the fact? But now he sounded nothing but indulgent and fond, as he spoke of his son and his 'ladyfriend'.

Keen to help her granddaughter settle in, Bel had asked Fox what she normally ate for breakfast, and the little girl had replied "Coco Pops!" which had necessitated Bel making a special trip to the campsite shop to procure the desired cereal, which Fox was now happily spooning up. Seeing her granddaughter after so long had melted Bel's frosty heart. She was clearly a very secure, loved little girl, which would indicate that Sophy had been a great mum to her. Bel was beginning to feel bad for the way she had judged Sophy all these years. Fox seemed to be settling in well, and her colourful possessions were already spread around the lodge, brightening up its beige interior - a rainbow striped cardigan draped over the back of an armchair; a pair of heart-shaped red sunglasses on the kitchen counter; a colouring book and a jumbo pack of felt-tip pens strewn all over the dining-table. It was as if she had already transferred some of the magic and colour of the circus into their lives. Meanwhile Fox had her own mobile phone, and Bel had heard her chatting to her mum earlier that morning. Bel hadn't yet asked Fox whether her mummy was likely to be popping over to visit anytime soon. Probably, the little girl did not herself know. And for the time being, Bel was perfectly contented just to have her granddaughter to herself.

Maggie frowned now. "Is there going to be enough room in here for everyone? I mean, little Fox is fine," she added hastily, watching the girl, who had moved on from Coco Pops to cartwheels, which she turned in the limited space on the balcony, her yellow dress flaring out around her like a sunflower. "She takes up hardly any room. But with two more adults, do we need to hire some extra accommodation or anything?"

"How about one of those glamping pods?" Lucy

suggested. "I'm sure there must be some available. How would you feel about renting one of those, Bear?" (This was her pet name for Barty.)

"Yes, no problem," Barty said. "I'm quite happy to stretch to a bit of extra accommodation to put Sebastian and Florence up."

Maggie frowned. "It seems a shame to stick your son out in a glamping pod, though, Barty." She could empathise with wanting to get closer to one's children. "You'll hardly see anything of him! How about Joe and Thomas share the glamping pod, I can go into Bel and Fox's bedroom in the lodge, and there will be a room free for your son."

"Oh, great, thanks very much, Maggie, sounds fantastic!" Barty enthused.

Listening to this discussion, Joe's face fell in dismay. "So I'm going to be moving out of the lodge, into a – a what was that you called it?"

"Glamping pod, yes," his son, Thomas, said, as if explaining it to a child. "It's a portmanteau word for 'Glamorous camping'. And it won't just be you, I'll be there too."

"Well yes I know, no offence Thomas you're wonderful company but even so -" Joe couldn't help but feel this relegation was a bit rich, especially as he himself was one of the main contributors to the sizeable cost of renting the lodge.

"Oh come on, Dad," said Thomas, who was

more used to roughing it. "It'll be a laugh! A lads' adventure." He looked at his father with mock-seriousness. "You'll have to promise me you won't fart all night though."

Joe said nothing, but shot his son a withering look, implying that his dignity had been insulted beyond repair.

*

They spent a lazy day around the holiday park; Barty and Joe did some fishing, and some of the others wandered off for a walk round the woods in the afternoon. In the evening, the Pizza Van visited the holiday park, so Lucy and Barty strolled down to collect wood-fired pizzas for everyone, after which delicious feast people retired to their sleeping quarters for an early night. New accommodation had already been procured for Joe and Thomas, and even though the new guests weren't due till the following day, Maggie and Bel decided the men might as well move out early, so there would be more room for little Fox to be comfortable that night.

"I feel like some kind of underclass," Joe said despondently, gazing into the gloomy confines of the glamping pod. "Banished from polite society." The floor was covered in a thin layer of carpet which had the texture of a brillo pad, and apart from that the place was completely unfurnished other than a low shelf with a kettle, and a couple of plug sockets. Structure-wise, the pod had curved sides that met at the top in a point, and made Joe feel as though he was going to be living in the hull of an upturned boat, rather like Shackleton's men when they got stranded in the Antarctic (*Endurance* was one of his favourite books ever). Joe had hoped he'd seen the last of this kind of accommodation when he'd left the Boy Scouts forty years ago.

"Lighten up, Dad," Thomas said, stamping energetically and repeatedly up and down on the foot-pump, while the airbed beside him slowly inflated. "We'll be closer to nature, might even see some cool birds or wildlife." Ever since he was little boy, Thomas had been crazy about nature and animals. Nowadays, there was an added poignancy to his interest, as he was aware how it was under threat due to climate change. But hopefully he could set these worries aside for a week, and just enjoy the holiday. OK, so the pod was very spare and basic, but personally, Thomas was just glad to be there. Since graduating from uni with a 2:1 degree in Maths, the only job he'd managed to get was on a conveyor belt picking garbage items - despite applying for a shedload of Data Scientist jobs. Combine that with student debt and the fact that he was saving up in the hope of one day finally leaving home and getting on the property ladder because he couldn't stand living at home with his parents and their shit show of a marriage, spending a few nights in a glamping pod with his father was the least of his worries. Tom was on the whole easygoing and tried to look on the bright side of things. You just had to live your life, he reckoned, and try to be happy. Sometimes he thought it was a shame his dad couldn't take a leaf out of his book.

CHAPTER 3

The next morning, Joe's mood had not improved. After an uncomfortable night on the double airbed with his son, he had a backache and sore, prickly eyes. First he went to refill their water container at the tap which was conveniently situated just a few yards from the pod. He went barefoot for this errand, and the grass was springy and warm underfoot, making him feel surprisingly happy and connected to the earth. Then he grabbed his wash bag and towel, slipped on his sandals and traipsed over the grass to the shower block. Joe's spirits began to lift further. The sun was already up, and there was something nice about feeling at one with nature, shoulders warmed by the sun, birds twittering around him, the fountain splashing in the lake nearby. Perhaps this was a glimpse of how his future life could be. A man from a nearby tent was outside cooking bacon on a barbecue as Joe walked past. The man was wearing a novelty apron depicting a woman's body clad in bra and knickers. "Good morning!" the man called cheerily, and Joe waved back.

The shower block was surprisingly good, spacious, modern and spotlessly clean. Joe turned the dial to the max and enjoyed a hot, powerful shower, then dried himself and dressed, feeling a lot better, his skin tingling pleasurably. On the way back, he saw that Barbecue Man and his wife were now sitting down in deckchairs tucking into their fry-ups. When Joe returned to the pod, he was enchanted to espy a little robin hopping about on the gravel beside the decking. His first thought was that Thomas would love to see it – but Thomas was still snoring on the Lilo – he was a boy who liked to sleep late – so Joe sighed and decided to pop over to the lodge instead. He was determined to make an effort and be sociable, to stop feeling like he was putting a dampener on everyone else's spirits.

However when he arrived at the lodge, everybody's attention seemed entirely focused elsewhere. Preparations were clearly underway for the arrival of the new guests later that day, Sebastian and Florence, as if they were some kind of royalty. Maggie and Bel were milling around, bossily giving orders to the others as bedding and possessions were shifted around the place. Barty had disappeared somewhere – probably the shitter, if he had any sense. Get some privacy while everyone else was distracted. At one point Maggie looked up from what she was doing. "Oh, Joe, it's you," she said, without interest – totally preoccupied.

"I wondered if there was anything I could do to help," he said, injecting brightness into his tone.

"Honestly, Joe," Maggie said, looking a little flustered and dishevelled from her efforts, "the most helpful thing you could do right now is get out from under our feet."

For some reason this made Joe feel sadder than he could have explained. Ah, well, what to do? Well, there was always that coursework to mark... but, sod the coursework! Quietly, Joe slipped away, back down the lodge steps and over to the family car parked just alongside. He unlocked the Rover, sat in the driver's seat and then, in a gesture of rebellion, ripped off the red neckerchief from round his neck, letting it drop onto his lap. Then he thought, sod it, no-one's going to miss me, and revved up the car and drove off. Joe zoomed off out of the Lakeside Park and around the narrow, winding leafy roads for ten minutes or so. As he mounted the brow of a hill, he impulsively threw his red neckerchief out of the window, which was caught on the breeze for a moment before being carried far away. Without the neckerchief, he felt considerably lighter, and sighed in relief. It was a Sunday, still early, and the roads were practically deserted. A couple of pheasants were startled by the approach of his car round a corner, and flew hastily away, with a heavy whirr of wings.

Finally, after driving for a while Joe came to a more built-up area, with a housing estate and a parade of shops. He pulled into a parking space to the rear of the shops and looked at what the parade had to offer. The usual suspects, a barber's shop, a convenience store, a fish and chip shop and there, at the end of the parade, something called the *Spice 'n' Dice* board game café.

As he approached the door he saw that the sign

was turned to 'Closed' and his heart sank. It was a Sunday, he should have known. However, just as he was about to walk away, a woman with colourful hair came towards the door and turned the sign round. She smiled at Joe through the glass, so that he knew it was OK to enter. A bell jangled as he opened the door and went in. He looked around him. It was a corner property, with two outside walls. There was a long window running the length of one wall. The place didn't really have the feel of a shop or café. Somehow it had the ambience of a room in an ordinary house; it was very cosy, and reminded Joe of the 1960s built house he had grown up in. Except that an ordinary room would not have been filled with tables and chairs, and would not have had a wall of shelves at the far end, stuffed to the brim with board game boxes of every design and colour. As he gazed in awe, the smell of fresh cake cooking in the oven rose to meet his nostrils.

"Morning," said the woman, smiling again. "I wasn't due to open for another fifteen minutes, but when I saw you here, I thought I might as well."

"Oh well it's jolly kind of you," Joe stuttered. Gazing at the woman, he saw that she was older than he'd initially thought, possibly mid-forties, close to his own age. A long attractive face, pretty rather than beautiful. Her look was spectacular, however: now that he had looked, he really could hardly take his eyes off her. She had a piercing in her septum, and another in her chin below her mouth. When she spoke there was an intriguing flash of silver from her tongue. The coloured hair was amazing – she had a full fringe that graduated through blue to grass green to lime green; the rest of the hair was pulled back in a ponytail, but strands of hair escaped at the sides in the same colour-scheme. She wore earrings shaped like lightning flashes, and winged eye makeup that exaggerated her dark eyes. The comfortable generous lines of her body meanwhile were clad in blue denim dungarees over a plain white t-shirt.

The woman gazed intently back at him, her scrutiny making Joe feel deeply embarrassed by his boring stone-coloured cargo shorts and the same blue checked shirt as yesterday which he had pulled on hastily as he left the glamping pod. At least he was thankful that he'd thrown the hated red neckerchief out of the car window.

There was the sound of a kitchen timer going off.

"Excuse me one moment," the woman said hastily. "I've just got to get a cake out of the oven." She went over behind the counter and rummaged around for a minute, before drawing out two steaming chocolate sponge cakes that smelt heavenly. Joe's empty stomach rumbled. The woman set the cakes on a cooling rack, dusted her hands off and then came back round the counter. "Sorry about that. Now, I'd better launch into my patter. My name's Rachael."

"My name's Joe," he replied. He was usually more formal than this, but as she'd offered her first name, he felt that he should reciprocate.

"Have you ever been to a board game café before?" Rachael went on. "It's not often people come in on their own," she added, glancing curiously at him. "Unless it's to one of our sessions. Anyway it's certainly not a problem. There's plenty of games just for one, or you can be both players if you wish! No-one's going to judge. Everyone can just vibe here and do their own thing."

"Sounds great," Joe said, surprised by how sincere he felt.

It was still early, and they were so far still the only two in the café. Rachael showed him to a table for two by the window and, feeling slightly awkward, he sat down in one of the seats. He looked around him, absorbing the entirety of the café. Different cakes were arranged all along the top of the counter, under clear plastic domes - even a mint choc chip one with piped rosettes of fluorescent green icing. Maggie would definitely have said that icing would have too many E numbers. And yet Rachael had gone to the trouble to make all of these beautiful cakes herself. It seemed he hadn't seen food so exciting since his childhood. This was the sort of place that made you feel anything was possible, even winding the clock back ten, twenty - even forty - years.

Still standing, Rachael looked down at him and said, "So, to explain how it works here, we charge a small cover charge of £2.50 per hour per person. This caps at £6 for up to 4 hours of fun! Any food or drink is added to a tab, and you pay for everything together at the end." Joe was a little startled by the complexity of the patter. He had almost forgotten she was operating a business here. Rachael went on, "I'm crazy about board games myself, so if you want any advice on choosing a game or how to play it, please ask away!"

"Well I –" Joe was going to say that he *did* used to like playing dungeons and dragons with his old school mates, and ask whether there were any board games along similar lines, but somehow the words froze in his throat and he said nothing.

Rachael frowned at him. "Are you OK?" She pulled out a chair and sat down opposite him at the small table.

"I don't know," he stammered. "It's just I-" Pathetically, ridiculously, Joe felt as if tears were close.

Rachael fetched a box of tissues from behind the counter, then sat back down. She lowered her voice, despite the fact that they were alone. "I was going to ask, if it wasn't too forward of me, what you were doing up and about so early on a Sunday, all on your own…"

Joe stared at her for a moment, and then suddenly it all came pouring out. Word upon word tumbled out of him. His hatred of his head master's job, his exhaustion, the pity he felt for some of the students, mired in poverty and family problems; the problems between him and Maggie, the way everything in life seemed so pointless and joyless. The fact that he was on holiday, but still couldn't help thinking about everything. The parasitic economic system, the feeling that everything was gloom and death, even the thing about the cows and the ice-cream for God's sake. "My God, that all got very deep, very quickly," he finished, blushing.

Rachael gave his hand a friendly squeeze across the table. "Oh, my love. This sounds like classic depression. You have a very negative spin on everything. But if you look at things in a different light, you'd see the ground we walk on isn't just decay and maggots – well, not in the pejorative sense, anyway. It's all about the beauty of nature, symbiosis, renewal. I've been in exactly the same place you are right now," she went on. "It is depression and it's a blackness that will cast a cloud over every part of your life. You should look into getting some counselling – sometimes you can get it through the NHS. Or else you can get it privately."

"OK," Joe said. "Maybe I'll look into that once I get back from the holiday..." His words trailed off feebly.

An anxious look crossed Rachael's face. "Hey, you're not thinking of doing anything stupid, are you?"

He shook his head. "No – I don't think so."

"Well, don't - *please*. It *does* get better, trust me – you just need to adjust and make some changes."

"You're right, of course," he said, sighing shakily.

"To be honest, I've been thinking that for a while."

"But what you say about life is true," she went on. "Living in our modern society *is* exhausting, every ounce of our being is manipulated or monetised permanently. We may wonder, what is the point in going through these socially constructed motions until death? Why should we do this monotonous lifeless shit until it's all over? We've been socially engineered to aim for the ideal nuclear family template we see in adverts and that could be where you're going wrong. Fuck the template and everything that goes with it!" She was quite quietly spoken, but spoke passionately. "Find your own route, like I've done. Try absolutely everything until you find something you love – I love working here – but I've travelled a lot in the past – Machu Picchu, the Grand Canyon, Rome – and I'm sure I'll get bitten by the travel bug again soon, and when I do I'll be happy to move on. Don't follow any authority, stick your fingers up to the government and anyone who tries to tell you otherwise. Live to be free, no constraints, no judgement and find what you truly enjoy doing and stick to it. I've lived in all sorts of places, but at the moment I live on a boat on the Wey and Arun canal. I'm never going to be rich, but personally a house in the suburbs with 2.5 kids and an office job would make me want to kill myself."

Joe laughed hollowly, thinking - too late, I've already been there, done that. And it hasn't all been bad, because I do love my kids.

"Sure," she went on, "it's not all roses, there will be plenty of highs and some real fucking lows but ride that wave!"

"Thank you," he said, when she'd finally finished speaking. "That's pretty inspiring. It really makes me believe there's something better out there."

She smiled self-deprecatingly, and, as he watched her, it struck him that beneath the coloured hair and the piercings, she was quite a modest person. Maybe even shy. "You must excuse me," she said, blushing. "I was putting my other professional hat on for a moment there. [*What did she mean by that, Joe wondered? And did professional people generally drop the 'F' bomb?*] You came here to play board games, and instead you got a monologue and life advice from me. I'm sorry."

"No," Joe said earnestly. "Please, don't apologise. All this is amazing, this place," he blushed, "the style you've got going is great – " He gestured helplessly with his hands. "It makes me feel like a right boring old fart," he added glumly.

Rachael's face broke into a broad smile. "You know what," she said. "You're not boring at all, just a bit lost. In fact, you're cute." She gestured upwards, towards his hair. "I love your eyes, and your smile. And your kind of helpless air."

Joe felt a kind of electric jolt go through him as he gazed into her dark eyes. This was crazy. He had never had such an instant connection with anyone before.

They seemed to lean towards eachother across the small table, her mouth was slightly open and again he saw the silver ball bearing that appeared to sit on her tongue. If I was to kiss her, Joe thought, I wonder what it would be like with the piercing. Suddenly he felt desperate to find out. Rachael closed her eyes and leaned towards him, and he was about to throw caution to the wind and kiss her when the bell on the shop door jangled, and they sprang hastily apart.

Rachael scrambled to her feet, and put on her best café proprietor smile. A group of two couples in their twenties had arrived, and Rachael showed them to a table, then went through her board game patter all over again. She fetched two games from the shelves, *Snakesss* and *Herd Mentality,* showed the people how to play them, then went to prepare their food and drinks order. On her way to the counter Rachael gave Joe a friendly wink, then a couple of minutes later she placed a freshly brewed cup of coffee on his table, along with a croissant and a board game called *The 7th Continent.* This was a game that could be played alone, as Joe soon discovered as he opened the box and became an early twentieth century adventurer, trying to lift a deadly curse in a distant, mythical land. Around him the café had gradually filled up with other customers. Rachael had a good way with people, Joe observed, but she was especially sweet with the young children. And whenever she got a free moment, Rachael popped over to see how he was getting on, and chat a bit more.

Joe hadn't had so much fun since playing dungeons and dragons, and he completely forgot about his 'normal life' until a couple of hours later, when his phone bleeped, heralding the arrival of a text from Maggie asking where he had got to, as Barty and Lucy were about to drive to the station to pick up his son Sebastian and his 'ladyfriend' (what even *was* a ladyfriend, Joe wondered? Was it the same as a girlfriend, or was there a subtle difference?).

As Joe went reluctantly to the counter to settle up, he noticed a pile of little business cards – *Licensed Therapist Rachael Garland* - next to the till. It was at this point he realised with a bit of a shock that Rachael did counselling as well as working at the café. Suddenly her earlier comment about her 'other professional hat' made sense. Joe's happiness faltered momentarily. Was her interest in him purely professional? Surely he could not have imagined the connection between them? But the warmth of her smile as they said goodbye helped to allay his fears.

"See you again soon, I hope?" she said softly, adding, "How long are you on holiday for?"

"A week," he replied, suddenly wishing it was longer.

She pushed one of her business cards across the counter to him. Turning it over, he saw that she had written 'Rachael' and her mobile number in pink biro on the back of it.

"So yes, I'll definitely be back," Joe told her. He

tucked the card into his pocket and drove back to the Lakeside Holiday Park feeling much lighter in spirits.

*

Lucy was feeling extremely apprehensive as she sat beside Barty in the car on the way to the station. She felt nervous meeting anyone related to Barty's previous life, the life that had not included her. As Barty sped through an amber light – "Amber gambler," he chortled delightedly to himself - Lucy raised a hand to her head, unsure about her new hairstyle. Fox, an affectionate little thing, had been fiddling with her hair earlier, while they had been sitting on the sofa together, the girl insisting on doing two little plaits, one either side of Lucy's face, which she then bound together so they formed a kind of crown atop her wavy blonde hair.

The impromptu hair styling had been done while Lucy and Fox were alone in the lodge. Some people had gone for a walk, Barty had gone for a drink and to read his book at the club house, and Lucy's dad had disappeared off God knows where. She herself felt quite chilled doing the 'baby-sitting'. Fox was the kind of child that made her wish more than ever to be a mother. Well-behaved, endearing and super-mature. The girl seemed quite enamoured of Lucy, too, and that morning had insisted on choosing Lucy's outfit for the day – a long, flowing floral dress that Lucy generally found a little frivolous for everyday wear. Fox herself was wearing a bright-pink sundress, and had done her own dark hair up in impeccable space-buns. "How are you finding it here, Fox?" Lucy asked gently, while the little girl was working busily away at the plaits.

Fox thought for a moment. "It's cool here, for a change. I like the ducks and Mouse." That was the name of the tortoiseshell cat that lived on-site. "I miss Mummy, of course…" Fox's words trailed off, and suddenly Lucy realised that she could hear the sound of gentle, snuffling sobs. She turned round to face the little girl, who dashed her tears impatiently aside, and said, "Oh no, now I've lost the end of the plait!"

"Sweetheart," Lucy murmured, reaching out and giving her a hug. "I don't think anyone realised you were feeling sad! I'm sure someone can take you back to your mum, this very evening if you want!"

Vigorously, Fox shook her head. "No. I don't want to do that. It's OK really, because we text eachother a lot, and it won't be long till I see her again." Fox wriggled out of the hug. "Now get back in position so I can finish your plait."

"Of course, miss." Suppressing a smile, Lucy made an effort to sit statue-like. She phrased her next question carefully. "It must be fun, living at the circus?"

"Yeah!" Fox replied enthusiastically. "I love it, especially our little caravan, just me and Mummy. And sometimes she lets me do training with her in the big top – she swings from the trapeze by her legs and holds me in her arms while I do a crab."

"Wow."

Fox's tone grew wistful. "I'm having fun here, but it will be nice to go back."

Lucy's stomach gave another little lurch of sympathy. "You must get through a lot of schools, moving around so much?"

"Yeah, but it's cool. When I go to a new school, everyone's always really nice to me. They can't believe that I actually live at a real circus!"

Lucy smiled. It seemed that Fox genuinely did love her life - but then, it was in her blood. The girl had been living in a circus since she was a baby. If only Lucy's own childhood had been more exciting, then she might never have felt the need to run away from home.

Shortly after her little chat with Fox, the others returned, hot and sweaty from their walk, with Barty in tow. The plaits, though beautiful, were pulling a bit. Lucy was about to pull the hair bobble out when Fox wasn't looking, but Barty stopped her. "You look like a woodland nymph, with your flowery dress as well," he told her approvingly. "Don't take it out just yet, Muffin." Oh well, she supposed it was harmless enough, if it made Barty happy. And it had been sweet of Fox to do it for her.

Now Barty's car was pulling up outside the tiny branch-line station. The late afternoon sun slanted into the car, making her feel too warm. Lucy felt her apprehension grow. Barty had his phone out, texting

Sebastian to tell him where they were. People began to emerge from the station. Lucy realised she didn't even have a clue what he would look like. She supposed he must resemble Barty in some way...

"Oh look, there they are!" Barty exclaimed excitedly, waving.

"Who - *them*?" Lucy was jolted by her first glimpse of Sebastian and Florence. They made a striking couple, the young man and woman walking towards them, each with a large, battered rucksack on their back. The boy, Sebastian, had dark curly hair flopping over his face, heavy-lidded blue eyes (bedroom eyes. Arrogant eyes?), and enviable bone structure. He was tall, broad shouldered but quite slim, she noted - a refreshing change from Barty's bulk, Lucy couldn't help thinking, disloyally. It struck her suddenly that she was far closer in age to Sebastian than to Barty himself. Seconds later she dismissed these thoughts, ashamed of herself. At least it was acceptable to approve of the pair's sartorial style. Son of Barty wore a white graphic tee with a slouchy black cardigan with flowers embroidered on it, teamed with camo trousers, while the young woman called Florence was wearing jeans with a strappy peach coloured top that showed off pale golden skin. She had an amiable round face, full cheeks and shoulder length dark blonde hair, which she wore slicked back off her face.

The thought of Barty being able to get away with an outfit like the one his son was wearing made Lucy want to giggle hysterically. The pair both looked slightly dishevelled, but pretty good considering they had spent the past few weeks in an underground tunnel.

"Hi Dad!" Seb and Florence crammed themselves and their rucksacks into the back seat of the car, one at each side.

"Seb, Florence, great to see you!" Barty boomed, swivelling round in his seat and shaking both their hands. "This is Lucy, my, er, significant other." Lucy felt hot under the collar as Sebastian clasped her hand, their eyes met, something flashed between them. "Sweet Echo, sweetest nymph that liv'st unseen," Sebastian murmured, staring at her.

"My thoughts *exactly,*" Barty exclaimed triumphantly.

"She *does* look rather beautiful," Florence agreed, to everyone's surprise. She had a warm, pleasantly husky voice.

"Is that quote John Milton?" Lucy asked, to cover her blushes at all the compliments. She vaguely recalled the line from her English A level studies.

Sebastian met her gaze again, and nodded, seeming impressed that she recognised the citation. Stuck-up, private school brat, Lucy thought mildly, while Barty revved up the car for the journey home. Sebastian was seated directly behind Lucy and she fancied she could feel his eyes boring into the back of her head, feel his warm breath on the back of her neck. Was she imagining it? Oh, for God's sake, she must be. The four of them made desultory conversation as the car sped along. Seb and, to a lesser extent, Florence were well-spoken, like Barty – the kind of way of speaking that Lucy herself tried to emulate these days, with limited success. Florence seemed friendly and chatty, and Lucy took to her at once. She was a nice looking girl, Lucy thought, observing her surreptitiously in the wing mirror. From time to time, Lucy had the suspicion that Florence was looking at *her,* too.

*

Ever since he had arrived back from the board game café, Joe had been unable to stop thinking about Rachael. He couldn't believe he had come so close to kissing her. Of course, he had not kissed another woman other than his wife through all the twenty-seven years of their marriage. The lightness he'd felt whilst with Rachael, however, only served to cast an even gloomier light on his relationship with his wife. He felt as though he needed to have a serious chat with Maggie, and soon. Once Barty and Lucy had set off to collect the new arrivals, he suggested to Maggie that they take a walk around the lake together. Looking slightly surprised, she agreed. "Just give me a minute." She reappeared seconds later, having changed out of her knee-length shorts into a pair of batik print trousers eccentrically patterned with roosters and improbably coloured fish.

"So," she began as they set out, "how's it going? Have you been sleeping well in the pod?"

Joe was momentarily wrongfooted. "What? Oh er well, no, not really, to be honest. The floor seems to be made of concrete. And I think the Lilo's got a slow puncture."

Maggie tried and failed to suppress a snigger. "Aw, diddums, are you sulking, Jojo? Is that why you went AWOL for so long today?"

"No," Joe said, blushing, "I, um, went for a long walk, to clear my head."

Maggie raised an eyebrow. "Then I'm surprised you feel like going for another walk now. I'd have thought you'd be exhausted."

Joe frowned. His stomach churned with guilt. Was she onto him? But, no, her expression beneath the fringe of mousy curls was as open as usual, brown eyes expectant and demanding rather than suspicious. That was good, because he certainly wasn't ready to tell her about Rachael yet. It was such early days, there was really nothing to tell. And yet he *had* to talk to her about the state of their marriage. "Maggie," he began tentatively, "you might have noticed I haven't been quite myself lately."

"Hmm, yes, something did seem a bit amiss," she replied. "But I just put it down to work getting you down, you know, the usual." They crunched along the gravel path beside the lake. There were roosting birds on the grassy banks, including a mother duck and her six ducklings. People were fishing from jetties, and the smell of barbecue smoke filled the air. "Lovely here, isn't it?" she murmured.

Joe could not bring himself to discuss their idyllic surroundings. He cleared his throat. "Maggie, can I ask you a question. How would you say things are between the two of us at the moment?"

Maggie looked baffled. "Fine," she said, sounding rather impatient. "At least, they are as far as *I'm* concerned. Why?"

He studied her intently. "Really, honestly, Maggie?" he asked gently. "You think things are fine as they are?"

"Yes!"

"But," he went on, struggling for words, "When was the last time we really talked, held hands, did anything fun?" At the moment, to him it really seemed they were just going through the motions.

Maggie stared at him. "Do you really *want* to do any of those things, Joe? If they're not spontaneous, if we have to force them?"

"Yes. No. I don't know." He paused. "But the thing is, if neither of us *want* to do those things, then surely something is wrong?" She said nothing, so he shrugged. "Anyway, the thing is, Maggie, I've been thinking, about where our, um, marriage is going, and -" he tried to think of the kindest way to put it, but failed. "Well, there's no easy way to say this, but personally I was thinking it might be time for us to go our separate ways."

Maggie looked utterly shocked. Joe's heart ached with pity for her. Despite the wreckage of their marriage, Maggie was still the person he had spent over twenty five years of his life with, the person he had once been deeply in love with. And of course, she was fundamentally a good person, one of the best. "What?" she was asking dully, "Get a divorce, you mean?"

"Well, er, not to put too fine a point on it, Mags, yes."

They had now walked halfway round the lake, and their own lodge was visible across the water, with the distant figure of Thomas sitting on the balcony, looking at his phone.

Maggie turned to him abruptly. "Are you having an affair? Is that it?" she demanded.

Joe's instinct was for instant denial. "No! Of course not." Well, strictly this was true, of course. Although his feelings for Rachael could not be denied, he did not even know how she felt about him yet. "I just think – there's no point continuing with something if it isn't working for us."

"Well it was working just fine for me! Oh, this is just typical of you, so selfish, perfectly timed so as to completely ruin our holiday –"

"Maggie, I'm *so* sorry. I know the timing sucks. But holidays are the only time we have to think about or discuss anything. Normal life is just too busy!"

If looks could kill, Maggie's expression right then would have left him stone cold dead. "You're doing my head in," she told him. "Just – just leave me alone for a bit. I need some time to process all this. Oh and by the way," she added, before storming off down the path ahead of him, "I'm glad you're in the bloody glamping pod, and that it's uncomfortable!"

CHAPTER 4

Dinner that night consisted of burgers and chips at the Club House. Delicious smoky burgers, soft brioche rolls, cheese, mayo, lettuce and tangy pickle, with hot salty French fries on the side. Afterwards, to celebrate the advent of the new arrivals, it was decided that they should go for a drink at the King's Head. The pub was located in Dragon's Green, a tiny village a five minute walk from the holiday park. Bel opted to stay behind with Fox. She was looking forward to putting her granddaughter to bed and reading to her from the Jacqueline Wilson book she had chosen especially for her. Lucy had mentioned to Bel about Fox's earlier tears, and Bel resolved to gently touch on that subject, too.

The remaining seven of them, Maggie, Joe, Lucy, Thomas, Barty, Sebastian and Florence, meandered in a straggly crocodile along the road that led to the village, as they went giggling and chattering excitably like a group of schoolchildren. Perhaps it was because of the new additions to the group that the dynamic had shifted and everyone felt effervescent. Lucy noted in mild disgust that her mother had got all silly and flirty, in a middle-aged woman kind of way. She even seemed slightly hysterical. "Ooh Barty," Maggie giggled, as they meandered along, "you didn't tell us your son was such a *dish!*" Then she threw a defiant look at her husband Joe, as if she was trying to needle him. Lucy wished the ground would open up and swallow her.

They soon arrived at the King's Head, where the party from the Lakeside Lodge commandeered a long wooden table inside the quaint, low-beamed pub, and Barty of course insisted on getting the first round in, foamy pints of shandy or beer for some, chilled glasses of white wine or pints of coke for others. The pub was lovely - they were very fortunate to have it on their doorstep, they commented to eachother: a picturesque seventeenth century building, the dark beams criss-crossing the ceiling, a huge stone inglenook fireplace adorned with horse brasses running the length of one wall; a crimson patterned carpet, and old oak tables and chairs.

Once they were all sitting down face to face, an awkward expectant hush fell. However the arrival of the drinks soon loosened people's tongues once again, and everybody wanted to know about Seb and Florence's experiences protesting in the Lambeth tunnels.

"The pair of you are very brave," said Maggie. "Although I must admit I'm a bit in two minds about these environmental protests. I *do* try and see both sides," she went on, "but I can't help noticing how the protestors are disrupting people's lives, glueing themselves to roads, trains, blocking petrol stations –

when the ordinary people are just stressed and trying to get to work."

To her surprise, it wasn't Seb or Florence who countered her argument but her husband, Joe, who spoke up. "Don't you *see*, though, Maggie," he said passionately, "it's the *Government* who are setting the protestors against the so-called ordinary people; it's *they* who are trying to make the protestors out to be annoying and disruptive, when really it's the government's fault for failing to heed the pleas of the protestors!" Maggie was quite taken aback - she had not known Joe had all this bubbling up inside him; she'd been unaware he felt quite so strongly about current affairs. She'd always thought his head was firmly stuck up in the clouds with the dungeons and the dragons.

"Couldn't have put it better myself, mate," Seb agreed, nodding approvingly at Joe.

"Yup. Divide and rule, that's the government's strategy," Florence chimed in.

"Point taken," Maggie conceded. "I take my metaphorical hat off to you both." She tipped back her glass and glugged back several millilitres of wine.

"Just remind me what was the particular protest you were involved with?" Joe asked, with a sideways glance at Maggie - he was slightly worried about the amount she was drinking, fearful she might do or say something reckless. "There seem to be so many going on at the moment – well it's hardly surprising, the country – or should I say the world – is a mess."

"We're protesting against the new railway," Florence told him. "Whose route is going to decimate a multitude of natural habitats. Right across the country."

"Yeah, I know, it's a disgrace, isn't it?" Thomas chipped in. "Hundreds of important habitats are under threat from the rail link. Ancient woodlands, veteran trees, wood pasture, old meadows, chalk streams and wetlands."

"That's right," Florence agreed.

"So you guys built these tunnels yourselves?" Lucy asked.

"Well, duh," Seb said, rather rudely.

Lucy was determined not to be put off by his attitude. "But how did you manage it? I mean, didn't anyone see what you were up to?"

"No, because we did it by night," Seb said. He fixed her with an intent blue gaze that made her heart flutter. "And we made a large kind of wooden construction out of pallets, to hide what we were doing."

Florence produced her phone. "Look," she said proudly, showing them a photo. Everyone gathered round, gazing at the screen in fascination. It showed a dilapidated, pallet-based structure, which looked rather like a rambling shed. It wouldn't win any awards for architecture, but then that was hardly the point. "The police and the council couldn't find the tunnels for ages," Florence said proudly. "It's because the entrances were very discreet, pretty small, only just big enough for a person to get in."

Joe shuddered. "God, it must've been pretty grim down there." He suffered from claustrophobia. Even the glamping pod was almost too cramped for his liking.

"Yes, how on earth did you chaps survive?" asked Barty. He raised his pint glass to take a large swig, his expensive wristwatch glinting in the light. "I mean, I'm jolly glad that you did, seeing as I'm rather fond of the pair of you, but, you know, it does make one wonder."

Florence shrugged. "OK, so the conditions were a bit cramped. It was quite hot down there too, and it got awfully muddy when it rained. But we did our best to keep our spirits up. We had chocolate, really nice cheese, kalamata olives... all stuff we'd stashed down there beforehand, knowing we'd need a few treats."

"Goodness. But even considering those toothsome delicacies, I still think it sounds hellish," said Barty.

"Well however bad it was," declared Sebastian, "it's nothing compared with the suffering caused by the ecological emergency."

"Hmm. You're right, of course," Maggie agreed. "But didn't you get terribly bored?" She herself got bored if she had to sit in a doctor's waiting room without a phone or a book for more than five minutes.

"A bit, but we did our best to keep ourselves amused," said Seb. "We had lights, and battery packs for our phones. And people were sketching, playing *Uno,* that sort of thing."

"Wow. I can't even begin to imagine what it was like," said Lucy, making mental notes, thinking what a fascinating article she could write about it for *The Witness.* But she wasn't just interested because of the article. The tunnel protests - and indeed Seb and Florence - genuinely fascinated her.

"I bet you were gutted to be evicted, weren't you?" Maggie asked.

"Fuck, yeah," Seb said. "But I can assure you we didn't go quietly. I chained myself to a steel pipe – it took them 25 hours to cut me free," he added with satisfaction. "You can still see the bruise on my wrist," he said, brandishing his wrist, to murmurs of sympathy. Lucy was one of the admiring onlookers. In spite of finding something objectionable in his character, Lucy couldn't help thinking how dashing Sebastian seemed, with his wild, curly dark hair – a hero from the Romantic era, a Heathcliff, not a Rochester – he was too handsome. A Heathcliff who came with his own Cathy in tow, she reminded herself firmly. Although she had yet to see any displays of affection between Seb and Florence – so far, they seemed to behave towards eachother simply as friends.

"I had to leave for the most mundane of reasons

in the end," Florence added gloomily, "because I'd run out of tampons, and they wouldn't give me any more."

"Bastards," Lucy murmured sympathetically.

"And of course we'll be summoned to appear in court in a few months' time," Florence went on. "Which is a bit of a drag."

"But we've had a couple of days to recover," Seb went on, "staying over at Florence's ma's place, and now we're ready to go again, aren't we Flo, whatever the next challenge may be!"

"That's right, we'll never give up," Florence declared. "We may have lost the battle, but one day we'll win the war! And you know what, the harder we make it for them, every time they want to do something that damages the environment, the more likely they are to think twice about doing it again!"

Lucy was impressed. In the past, she'd often wondered how protestors could find it in them to care so passionately, when it often seemed their efforts were doomed to failure; in the face of big business and the machinery of the state. But she found Florence's words deeply inspiring.

"When progress is destruction," Seb added, raising his pint glass, "we need an interruption. When the law says it's OK, it's time to disobey!"

"Yeah, right on, mate!" cheered Thomas.

Joe was also inspired by Seb and Florence's spirit of rebellion. He felt himself urged on to greater things.

They all clinked their glasses together, as if drinking a toast.

"Stirring stuff," Maggie agreed enthusiastically, taking another big sip of white wine. "Although, to be honest, you're both looking a bit underfed after so long in that tunnel! We'll have to make sure we feed you up on this holiday! I'm in awe of your level of commitment, though," she added. "And such a worthy cause, I'm sure everyone would agree."

Sebastian raised an eyebrow. "Not too sure about *everyone*. Dad talks a good game, but he doesn't really give a shit about climate change, do you Dad?"

"What?" Barty glanced up from his pint, then sideways at Lucy, looking embarrassed. "Sebastian, how can you say such a thing?" he stuttered. "Of *course* I care!"

Lucy raised an eyebrow. She thought it was a bit mean of Sebastian to keep needling his father in this way. But this didn't stop her feeling strongly drawn towards Sebastian - if only they didn't both already have partners. And if only *her* partner didn't happen to be his father!

Barty drained his pint glass. "Who's getting the next round in? I'm parched."

Thomas looked sheepish. "Not me. I'm skint, I'm afraid."

Lucy laid her hand on her brother's arm. "Poor Thomas," she murmured protectively to the assembled group. "He's always skint."

Barty looked at Thomas in apparent bafflement. "But how come? You do have a job, don't you?"

"Well yes I do," Thomas explained, "but the pay's pretty abysmal."

Barty's brow creased in consternation. "Well it must be at least a *reasonable* amount at least. I know for a fact that the minimum wage has increased recently."

"I know," Thomas said patiently, "but meanwhile, the price of everything has gone up *more* than the minimum wage."

Barty looked as if he was going to say something else, but Lucy silenced him with a single glance. "That's enough, leave my brother alone." Meanwhile Seb was watching the exchange with interest.

"Actually, Thomas is absolutely right," Joe chipped in. "People are really struggling at the moment. At the school where I teach, whole families are going hungry."

"Now this is what I don't understand," Barty said, leaning forward across the table. "How people can go hungry when you can get a bag of pasta for – how much is pasta, Lucy?"

"About 80p," she said. "But how would you like to just eat plain pasta every day, Barty? With no protein or vegetables? It would just be tasteless, and un-nutritious. Not to mention bloody depressing."

Because she'd had a drink, the swear word was out of her mouth before she knew it.

Maggie eyed the confrontation anxiously. Despite the fact that she'd recently knocked back a large glass of wine, she could see the potential for things to escalate into a full-blown slanging match. She stood up, and just as she would with an unruly class at school, clapped her hands to get everyone's attention. "OK, people!" she announced, in her best teacher voice. "*I'll* get the next round in. Now, who would like another drink?"

*

They stayed quite late at the pub, and were all quite merry by the end of it, probably waking half the village up when they walked home. Thomas and Sebastian had bonded over a shared love of nature and conservation, and as a result they were now best buddies. "There's a nature reserve about 20 minutes' drive from here," Thomas said eagerly, recognising an ally. "Apparently the reed beds are good for warblers and water rails. I fancy going and having a look round it tomorrow. What do you think, Seb?"

Seb nodded enthusiastically. He was definitely up for it, though sadly when the following day dawned bright and sunny as usual, there weren't that many other takers for the trip. Maggie wanted to have use of the Rover to take Bel and Fox into Haughton to buy the little girl some more reading books and also a pair of good quality walking shoes. Barty wanted to stay behind and work on his long overdue biography of John Donne. Joe wanted to stay behind as well – there was something he wanted to have a word with Barty about, and if he had time he also thought he might text Rachael on the quiet. He was quite looking forward to having the glamping pod to himself, in which to message her in privacy. Florence said she thought the nature reserve sounded fun and would join Seb and Thomas.

"I can drive us there," Sebastian said. "You'll be OK to lend me your car, won't you, Dad?" It wasn't exactly a question, more of a demand. "Are you going to join us, Lucy?"

Lucy blushed and said that, OK, yes she would. She felt vulnerable in the slouchy hoodie she had put on over her nightie to have breakfast, and quickly followed Barty into their bedroom to get ready for the day. She felt that she needed some armour on before she could face the glamorous Sebastian.

"Ah yes, Muffin," Barty began, the second she had closed the bedroom door behind them. "There was something I wanted to talk to you about. No biggie," he added, seeing that she was looking anxious. "You see, the thing is, it might be necessary for us to go back to London a couple of days early."

Lucy felt her heart plummet in disappointment. "Oh? Why's that?"

"Well you see the thing is, these people from *Hello* magazine want to do an article about me, take some photos of me at home, get some nice shots of the flat, etc. It'll be just the ticket for my political career."

"Hmm. I don't get it, though," Lucy frowned, as she faced him across the bed. "Why does that have to include me? Why can't I just stay here and enjoy the holiday for a bit longer?"

"Because you're my partner, Muffin," Barty explained, as if to a child. "The photos will look nicer if you're in them too, maybe in the kitchen cooking a meal or something, or showing the two of us relaxing on the sofa together. It will all help to build up my image as a modern, reliable, man, a decent partner, and it'll help to build my profile with the public."

Lucy felt the annoyance rise within her. "Barty, I'm not some kind of domestic accessory, some little wifey who stays at home while her big macho partner goes out into the world, putting it to rights!"

Barty sighed heavily. "Come on now, my sweet. I thought we agreed that we'd be partners in all our endeavours, and that if one of us needed the other's support in their career, they would gladly give it." His big, noble face looked hurt and confused.

"Yes well that's all very well," she said crossly. "But it seems to be a bit of a one way street at the moment!"

She sat heavily down on the dressing table stool, angry and embarrassed. She felt mortified – was that really how Barty saw her, as the little woman who did the cooking while he went out and built his career? Lucy did regret having raised her voice now, aware as she was that Sebastian and Florence's bedroom was nextdoor to theirs and the walls of the lodge were pretty thin. All the previous night, Lucy had felt strangely on edge, inexplicably cringing at the prospect that any sounds of passion might emerge from the nextdoor room – though in the event she had heard none. Similarly, she was glad to find that Barty had been already asleep and snoring by the time she had put on her nightclothes and got into bed, and that there would be no chance of lovemaking that night.

"I'm going to have a shower now," she announced, coming back to the present, before Barty could attempt to offer an olive branch. And she slipped quickly out of the room.

The shower was hot and therapeutic, banishing thoughts of the disagreement. After she'd dried off, Lucy went to find Fox, to see if she'd like to do her hair again. She discovered the little girl on the grass just outside the lodge. "Great idea!" said Fox, who'd been busy practising her cartwheels and somersaults, while pop music played tinnily on her phone. "If I do loads of plaits while your hair's still wet, when your hair's dried you'll have lots of lovely curls, just like mine!"

"You clever girl," Lucy said. "I'll have to owe you an ice-cream for this – or several."

"Hmm." Fox thought about it. She plastered her sweetest smile to her face, a smile that seemed to know it was pushing its luck. "Could you take me into town and buy me some make-up instead?"

"Ooh I don't really think that's a good idea, sweetheart - your skin is too young and beautiful to be plastered in make-up. How about I buy you a really pretty bunch of flowers instead?"

Thankfully this idea seemed to appeal to Fox. Once the plaits were done, Lucy thanked her profusely and returned to her bedroom. To her relief, it was now empty – Barty must have gone off somewhere. She selected another long, floaty dress to wear to the nature reserve; for now her tailored suits and blouses would have to remain neglected in the wardrobe. She paired the dress with her flat, leather, gladiator sandals. Lucy's hair dried quickly in the heat, and Fox was absolutely right; once it was dry and she'd removed the plaits, she thought fancifully and rather vainly that maybe Sebastian would say – seeing as he liked arty comparisons and had quoted poetry at her the other day – that she looked like a Botticelli.

In fact, Lucy was quite disappointed when the four of them got into the car to leave for the nature reserve and no such comment was forthcoming.

No-one said much on the journey; they were all just chilling out, enjoying the scenery. At the end of the twenty-five minute drive they emerged from the car to find a vast tranquil lake scattered with lily pads, surrounded by bullrushes and reeds. To one side was a picturesque disused water mill. The place was run by volunteers and they paid their money to go in.

The four of them, Lucy, Thomas, Sebastian and Florence, wandered through the reserve, silently, drowsily, as if in a dream. Paths were cut through the full lush greenery everywhere, it was the height of summer and everything was in full bloom. Thomas made extremely slow progress. He stopped to look at every plant and insect they passed, to photograph it and then attempt to identify it with his app. "Oh, that's a Silver Washed Fritillary," he would say. "That plant is Sneezewort." Florence hung on his every word, fascinated to learn what everything was. Meanwhile, Lucy and Seb began to ease ahead. There seemed to be no need for communication between them. It was as if they could read eachother's minds, and were in perfect harmony as they moved along, twigs and leaves crunching underneath their feet. Lucy was mesmerised by her attraction to Sebastian, who today was wearing a bright blue shirt buttoned up to the neck, untucked over black jeans. The shirt looked stunning with his eyes. And yet, she reminded herself, he was more than just a pretty face. He was a man of principles, too.

"You know," she said, looking at him, "I can't help admiring you for spending all that time in that tunnel."

He smiled. "Try not to admire me too much. The fight is not about individuals, it's about societal collapse and the death of millions. If that rail route goes ahead, it will damage so many wildlife sites and places of scientific interest. Sure, the company say they will plant trees and re-create habitats but that's just bull, it's never going to compensate for what they've destroyed."

Lucy listened raptly. "My brother's into conservation, stuff like that," she said. "But I used to think it was boring. I was a self-centred little thing," she finished shamefully. "Although I guess I had my own problems." She hoped he wouldn't ask what they were, and he didn't.

"Well, it's never too late to have a change of heart," Sebastian said, smiling across at her as they continued to walk.

After a while, the parked forked off to the right, leading down a slight slope to a bird-watching hide. A sign on the outside of the long wooden building said, "Quiet, Please." Wordlessly, Lucy followed Sebastian into the dark, gloomy interior, the only light coming from the long, slit-like openings for viewing the birdlife. The long wooden benches held a scattering of occupants, retired types, mostly men with one or two women, many in possession of huge-lensed camouflaged telescopes, training them on the birdlife with deadly seriousness.

Sebastian and Lucy entered into the hushed atmosphere, sitting down side by side at the far end of one of the benches. They were so close that their bodies were touching. Lucy knew she was entering dangerous territory, but she felt reckless, still angry with Barty for expecting to cut short her holiday at the drop of a hat. Her heart-rate sped up at Sebastian's proximity and the awareness of his smell, a mixture of lemony cologne and pheromones. Lucy tried to distract herself by gazing out of the aperture at the view. The view was a stretched oblong of green, comprising a line of bird feeders with various garden birds hanging off them – blue-tits, chaffinches, nuthatches - and a plump pigeon waddling comically about underneath.

"I'm not really in the mood for birdwatching. Shall we count shoulders?" Sebastian whispered, his breath warm on her neck.

She turned to him in bemusement. "What do you mean?" she whispered back.

"Look – one, two –" he touched his own two shoulders, "three" he touched her shoulder nearest to him, "four" – he snaked his arm around her shoulders and pulled her close. Lucy giggled, and one of the retired birdwatchers shushed crossly from further down the line. Then Seb murmured, "Oh, what the hell," and kissed her; it was thrilling in the darkness of the hide. The kiss got quite passionate; Lucy wondered what the hell she was doing, as he ran his hand through her long hair – she knew she was behaving like a shit. Over her shoulder she caught a glimpse of an elderly birdwatching couple staring their way and tutting. It was a bit of a passion-killer, and she pulled away from Seb.

"Come on," Sebastian murmured, taking her hand

and pulling her to her feet. They emerged from the hide, back into the sunshine, walking separately now, both seeming rather dazed. It was as if they were back in the real world, amongst greenery and blue skies, and what had happened in the hide was just a dream.

Sebastian took her hand again, then turned her wrist to inspect the little flower tattoo there. "Cute," he said, stroking it with his finger.

"Thanks," she murmured. "I'm not quite sure what happened in that hut place," she went on.

They were walking along the path, holding hands, Lucy fervently hoping that Thomas and Florence would be too slow to catch up with them.

"I know, right?" Seb agreed, shaking his head. "It's really weird, when I think about it."

"You mean, because I'm in a relationship with your father?" Lucy asked, suddenly defensive.

"Yes." His expression turned serious. "I mean, Lucy, I don't know how you *can*. The man is morally bankrupt and a prize shit."

Lucy stared at him in surprise, that he would talk that way about his own father. "That's a little harsh, isn't it?" she accused him. "I mean, I know no-one's perfect, but your dad clearly thinks the world of you! He runs round after you, collecting you from the station, paying for this holiday for you, but all you seem to do is make sarcastic comments about him!" Lucy didn't really feel that much animosity towards

Seb; she was quite enjoying the cut-and-thrust of the bantering.

"He deserves it," Seb shot back. "He treated my mother like shit, trading her in for a younger model, discarding her like a piece of rubbish –"

"Oh God," Lucy murmured, as the realisation hit home. "That sucks." She could see the pain in Seb's eyes, as for the first time she got an inkling of the trail of destruction Barty had left in his wake.

"I know, right," Sebastian said. "And now he's moved on *again,* to you, the jammy git."

"What do you mean?" she frowned.

"I mean, he's old, and gross, and you're young, and beautiful."

Lucy shivered with pleasure at the compliment. But also, instinctively, she came to Barty's defence. "He's not 'gross'! And OK, so he's older than me, but you're younger than me, so what's the difference?"

"Yes, but there's only about, what, a year or two between us? I'm twenty-three, and you're -"

"Twenty-four. Anyway," she went on quickly, "age doesn't matter. Barty and I suit eachother well. We do the same work, and both enjoy it. And we enjoy the finer things that we can buy with our salaries... I – I love him." She paused. "Or at least, I thought I did." She gulped. "The thing is, when I'm with you, I kind of can't help myself."

"Ditto." Sebastian stared intently at her as they

walked along. He raised a hand to shield his eyes from the sun. "You know what, you look like that painting by Botticelli."

Lucy felt her heart rate quicken. "*The Birth of Venus*?" she asked, to cover her excitement and discomposure that the compliment had finally arrived.

Sebastian laughed. "No, because then you'd be clad in nothing but a seashell. I mean, *La Primavera,* spring."

Lucy blushed at her faux-pas. "Oh yes, of course." How was she expected to keep up with him, for heaven's sake? He'd had a fancy private education – Barty had told her that himself, complaining about what it had cost him - whereas she'd gone to a humble comprehensive school. (Even if they *could* have afforded a private school, her parents would have chosen a state school, believing that it was good for people of all walks of life to mingle together.)

"What about Florence?" she asked him now.

"Oh, she's just a friend. We've known eachother since we were kids."

Lucy raised an eyebrow. "Friends with benefits?"

"Lucy!" he laughed. "What a thing to ask!" But he didn't answer the question.

They came to a stop in a little clearing. Lucy leant back against the solid trunk of an oak tree, and as he leaned over her, she squirmed under his scrutiny.

Seb stroked a finger deliberately hard over her cheek, removing some of the thick make-up she coated herself in, saying, "You don't need this. Skin is skin. It doesn't have to be perfect, it's beautiful anyway."

"Oh please, don't patronise me," she murmured, feeling her face flood with heat. Her skin, for God's sake. The one thing she was self-conscious about. Sebastian was so self-confident, it bordered on arrogance.

Suddenly they heard feet tramping through the undergrowth towards them, and sprang apart. They heard familiar voices, then Thomas and Florence emerged from a path through the trees. "Oh *there* you are, guys!" Thomas said, mildly indignant. "You could have waited for us!"

"Sorry mate," Sebastian drawled. "But you were taking too bloody long."

Thomas looked sorry for himself. "I wanted to get some refreshments, then come back and do a bit more plant identification afterwards!"

"Oh, poor Tom," Lucy said appeasingly. "Come on then, let's go and grab a bite to eat now."

The four of them headed back to the Heron's Rest café, where they sat outside at the faded grey wooden tables, bordered with pretty flower beds and fragrant lavender bushes, and enjoyed pots of tea and scones with clotted cream and strawberry jam. Lucy felt wracked with guilt whenever she glanced across at Florence's sweet face. Meanwhile she could hardly bring herself to look Sebastian in the eye.

CHAPTER 5

Joe steeled himself for the task he'd set himself. He knew he should take the opportunity, while everyone else was out. The door to Barty and Lucy's bedroom was half-open, and through it, Joe could glimpse Barty sitting on the bed, frowning furiously through his spectacles, while he typed away on his laptop. He was quite a sight in his shorts and today's choice of Hawaiian shirt, a lurid orange and yellow number featuring a sunset and silhouetted palm trees. His chunky legs and sandalled feet stuck straight out on the bed before him. Joe had made sure that the two of them had the lodge to themselves before deciding to make his approach. He coughed and knocked on the half-closed door. Barty's head jerked abruptly up, then he noticed Joe and smiled. "Well, hello my old mucker. Come on in. What can I do for you?"

Joe crept tentatively into the bedroom, feeling a bit uneasy to be on this private territory which his daughter also shared. "Barty," he began, "this is a rather delicate matter but, well, there's something I'd like to ask you about."

"Oh, really?" Barty pushed his half-moon spectacles up onto his head, ruffling his russet hair in the process. His blue eyes blinked myopically at

Joe. "Take a seat, old chum," he said, whacking the mattress beside him. "Ask away."

Joe felt slightly awkward approaching Lucy's partner about something like this, but as his attempts at communicating with Maggie seemed to have stumbled, he was at a loss as to where else to turn. He felt a little desperate. The colour and magic that had entered his life along with Rachael was in danger of being swallowed up into the darkness once again. And Barty seemed a good option. Joe lowered himself delicately onto the edge of the bed beside Barty. He ran a nervous hand through his salt-and-pepper hair, and cleared his throat.

He was about to speak when Barty interrupted him, his face slightly reddened. "This – er – wouldn't happen to be about your daughter, and the fact that she and I had words earlier..."

Joe was completely wrongfooted. "What? No."

Barty looked intensely relieved. "Oh, phew. Jolly good. I just thought she might have put you up to having a man-to-man chat with me, that's all."

"No." Dismissing any curiosity as to what was going on between Barty and Lucy, Joe tried to regain the vibe he had had going before, to get into the serious yet tactful frame of mind needed to approach Barty on a certain sensitive subject. "Bart," he began again. "You're a man of the world," he began.

"Ye-es."

"So. I was just, er, wondering whether you would have any advice for a man who was thinking about divorce?"

"Gosh – " Barty looked utterly stunned. "You mean you and Maggie? But - but why would you want to do a thing like that?"

Joe hung his head. "Because it's over, Barty. Dead. It's going nowhere between us."

"Oh goodness me. Well I'm jolly sorry to hear that, old man." Looking up, Joe saw Barty narrow his eyes at him shrewdly. "Have you got another filly on the side, is that it?"

Joe blushed. "No, no," he said hastily. He hated to think of Rachael as 'another filly'. It seemed so sordid.

"Ah. OK."

"But I've had enough. I hate my life. I want to make a fresh start."

"Woah, steady on there, old boy." Barty looked slightly taken aback at the strength of Joe's language. "Is teaching getting you down, is that it? All those little brats at the school? Perhaps early retirement would be the thing. Another five to ten years or so, and you could call it quits. Spend your time in your garden, growing sunflowers."

Joe shook his head. "No, it's more than just that. I want to get out – completely out – of the rat-race. Now." He paused. "Barty, do you think it would be possible for me, with, say £30,000, to buy some sort of run-down house in rural Wales or somewhere?"

Barty burst out laughing, a deep belly laugh, throwing back his head in mirth. "Oh, good heavens, no!" It made Joe feel as if he had shrunk to about two feet tall. "No, it's just not feasible, Joseph, that's nowhere near enough money. Look," he went on, "this whole thing is preposterous. Are you really sure you've thought this through? Throwing away everything you've achieved for yourself - your home, your career, your family?"

Joe felt slightly confused by Barty's attitude. "I don't understand, Barty. You're twice-divorced yourself, and you seem to have come through it OK. In fact, I might venture to say that you seem pretty happy?"

"Yes, but has it really been *worth* it, my friend? Was it really worth the hassle?"

Joe wondered if he was being patronised. Glancing around the room, his eyes fell on the Patek Philippe watch, discarded on the dressing-table by the open window. Barty was wearing another watch today, a Rolex, almost as smart and probably almost as valuable. The Patek Philippe's golden face glinted in the sun that poured in through the window. For heck's sake, Joe thought. Anyone could steal the watch lying there, and would Barty even notice it was gone?

"Sure," Barty was going on, "I've been through two divorces, but do I regret it? Yes, quite possibly. Jolly expensive business, too. And you have to think about the children. I mean, it would be terribly unsettling to Lucy and, er, er, Thomas."

"I do," Joe said, "and it's really admirable of you to have Lucy's best interests at heart. But - but your Sebastian seems to have turned out OK. Though I'm not saying it was always easy for him..."

"No it wasn't, not at all, and I feel terrible for that! Look," Barty went on, confidingly, "take my advice, pal, stick with what you've got. Everyone else does and gets by, what makes you think you're any different, eh?" He nudged him jokingly, but Joe thought he sounded as though he really meant it.

"OK, well thanks for your advice, Barty," Joe said, rather shortly. "Oh, and I'd rather you didn't breathe a word of this to anyone."

Clenching his fists as he got up off the bed and hurried from the room, Joe felt angry, and indignant. He was appalled by the man's attitude. It was as if Barty was saying it's OK for the likes of Barty - upper middle-class, privileged, the class that had all the power – to leave their partner and start a new life, but not for Joe, part of the downtrodden, plebeian masses. Joe sighed and shook his head. He *had* thought of Barty as a friend. But Lucy's intended husband had certainly gone down in his estimations that day.

Joe stomped off down the steps of the lodge, feeling the low mood threatening him once again. What if Barty was right, though? What if there *was* no point in trying to change your life, and you just had to stay shackled to the same old routine until you died? He shook his head, trying to dislodge the gloomy thoughts. He sought for something buoyant to cling to, like a drowning man looking for a life raft. Then as Joe made his way back to the pod, he suddenly remembered it - the business card Rachael had given him. His heart leapt. Joe reached into his pocket, withdrawing the card with her phone number written in pink on the back. Then he got out his phone and composed a text to her. Surprisingly, he had no trouble at all in wording the text; the feelings just seemed to flow out of him. *'Hi Rachael, it was great to meet you yesterday. Would you like to meet up again sometime? X'* The kiss was added, somewhat daringly, as an afterthought.

He had not even had time to unlock the door of the pod when the reply came back. *'Love to! How about today if you're free? The café's closed on Mondays.'*

'Perfect!' Joe put, then hesitated. Maggie had taken the Rover, which meant he was stranded. *'I'm without transport, I'm afraid.'*

'Where are you staying?' Rachael replied. *'I'll come and get you.'*

She arrived twenty minutes later in a battered cream and burgundy 2CV. As soon as he saw her, his spirits lifted, and he pushed the irritating conversation with Barty to one side. Rachael looked amazing as ever, a brightly coloured beacon of hope, her hair pulled back in a ponytail which emphasised the lime and forest green fringe. She wore cute dangling earrings in the shape of little pigeons, and was clad in a mustard top and some sort of black pinafore thing which fitted comfortably to her curves. Her face lit up when she saw him, and he smiled back. Quickly, they made a plan - they would drive to Crow's Heath, a village to the west of Haughton, have a look round the YMCA charity shop there – which Rachael said was a really good one - and then maybe find a café to get a spot of lunch.

Joe knew Maggie liked charity shops, but he himself rarely went in them. When he'd been growing up, his parents had been of the opinion that wearing pre-owned clothes was somehow unsanitary, and a stigma of poverty. Fortunately, people seemed to have a much more sensible attitude nowadays. Charity shops seemed to be popping up everywhere lately, symptomatic no doubt of the state of the economy, coupled with the need to recycle. Joe's gloomy thoughts threatened again, but he shoved them aside. Uncertain at first, Joe stepped inside the premises and soon found himself happily browsing the rails of clothing, while an old CD of 80s music blasted out over the sound system. His spirits lifted. This was great. Charity shops were actually a wonderful thing, he realised. Good for the environment plus they didn't feed the corporate greed machine.

Rachael made a bee-line for a dress she liked, with a swirly skirt and a fabric patterned with orang-utans. Meanwhile, Joe found himself drawn to a pair of tan lace-up work boots that seemed to be in his size. He picked out a couple of items of clothing, too, and then he had an outfit. Slim black jeans, a black Armani suit jacket (what a find!) and tan suede boots. He showed Rachael, saying, "Maybe not the most sensible clothing for summer, but I like their vibe."

Rachael laughed. "Why don't you try them on? There's a changing room over there." She pointed to a little curtained cubby hole in the corner.

In the changing room, Joe shed his boring shorts, slipped on the jeans and jacket and laced himself into the boots. The clothes all smelt of soap powder, and Rachael had mentioned that everything in the shop was freshly washed. He looked in the mirror, and wasn't sure. His reflection didn't even look like him, for starters. He felt a little embarrassed. Joe stuck his head out of the curtain, careful to keep the rest of his body concealed. "Rachael!" he hissed, praying none of the other shoppers would notice him. Rachael abandoned the rail of clothes she was flicking through, and came over. "What do you think?" he asked her. Tentatively he drew back the curtain.

Rachael whistled under her breath. "I like it! The only fly in the ointment is," she frowned, "that checked shirt doesn't really go. Hang on, I'll grab you a t-shirt." Seconds later she was back with a dark grey t-shirt on a hanger. Joe closed the curtain and changed again.

A couple of minutes later, he was ready for

another reveal. He stood back proudly for Rachael to admire. The fit of the jacket was loose and elegant (much better than the cheap polyester suits he wore for work) - it seemed to set off his salt-and-pepper hair, making it look distinguished. The jeans and boots were just right, too. He raked a hand through his hair, sweeping it back.

"Wow," she said. "You know what, you look a bit like Steve Carell – now he's a silver fox, of course. Have you seen how good he looks lately?"

Joe blushed. "Oh – well, thanks. I think."

Joe liked the outfit so much that he wished he could keep it on. However, the last time he'd done something like that was when he'd been aged about five, and had insisted on wearing his new shoes home from the shoe shop. As he was now a grown adult he decided this sort of behaviour wasn't appropriate any more and reluctantly got changed back into his old clothes.

"Ooh, who's your handsome new friend, Rachael?" asked the manageress, when they came to pay. She was in her late fifties, and had long blonde frizzed hair, and lots of make-up, applied with more exuberance than accuracy.

Rachael smiled. "Hi, Mimi. This is Joe. Joe, I used to work here for a bit, before I started at the board game café."

"I *say* friend," Mimi went on, "though for all I know he could be your hot new beau."

"Calm yourself, Mimi," Rachael said good-naturedly, "we're just friends."

Thankfully the manageress seemed satisfied with that, turning her attention instead to her pair of middle-aged male assistants, telling one of them to take the hangers out of their purchases and another to fetch a big bin bag.

"Crikey, looks like you're buying a whole new wardrobe!" chortled the one fetching the bag, a greasy-haired man in a long leather raincoat, a bit like the one worn by Neo in the Matrix.

"Ooh, this used to be mine, I think!" said another, picking up the orang-utan patterned dress and twirling around with it.

"Shut up, Dave, you silly bugger," said the first one.

"Now, now, gentlemen, watch your language in front of us ladies," Mimi said with exaggerated reproof.

"What ladies?" said the one in the leather coat. "I can only see one lady, and it's not you."

"Charming!" Mimi raised her pencilled-on eyebrows at Joe so he smiled obligingly back, and even managed a chuckle. "That'll be £27 please, darling," she said. "I take it you're paying for Rachael's as well?" she added with a wink at Rachael.

Back out in the street, Joe clutched his bag of clothes possessively. He was feeling ridiculously excited about them.

They had jacket potatoes and salad for lunch in a nearby café, where they somehow started a conversation about what their favourite kids' programme had been when they were younger. They both agreed to a secret fondness for *Danger Mouse*. Then they got onto other subjects. She told him that she had a grown-up daughter from a previous relationship. The daughter, Petal, was an aid worker on the island of Lesbos, helping refugees. Joe expressed admiration at this. Somehow he skirted around the subject of his own family life, and, shamefully, the existence of Maggie.

Afterwards Rachael drove him back to the camp site. They breezed along in the 2CV, up and down the gentle slopes. "Would you like to come and see my pod?" Joe asked impulsively, as the car wound its way through the leafy lanes. "It's quite an interesting piece of construction, boat-shaped, quite beautiful really - and everyone else is out at the moment."

Suddenly Rachael's face fell. "Joe," she said, darting a brief glance at him before turning her attention back to the road. There was a little crocheted bumble bee dangling from the rear-view mirror, which danced about with the motion of the car. "This outing has been really fun and all, but you did mention you were married, didn't you? What about your wife?" She chewed on her bottom lip, looking anxious.

All of a sudden Joe felt sick, as if a pin had been raised to the balloon of his happiness. If he was a decent person, he thought, he would tell Rachael the truth right now, about how Maggie had not reacted favourably to the idea of a divorce. He owed that much to Rachael, and to Maggie. However he was weak, despicable, and couldn't bear to deal a death blow to their blossoming relationship. "It's over between us," he heard himself blurting out. "Dead." He seemed to recall using very similar words earlier, to Barty.

Rachael looked concerned. "God, I'm sorry. That sucks, for you guys. So have you talked to your wife about it? How does she feel about the situation?"

Joe gazed across at Rachael, at her lovely face, in which the kindness added to the beauty. The thought of her dropping him off at the pod and then driving away, leaving him on his own once again, seemed almost unbearable. He was a terrible person, he knew. Weak-willed. And he hated himself. "Yes," he heard himself lying. "My wife and I have spoken about it and she feels the same as me. We're going to get a divorce."

Rachael gave a sharp intake of breath. "I see. Well, that does put matters into a different perspective…"

*

Meanwhile, Bel, Maggie and Fox were getting on well in the town centre. The three of them chattered away like old friends – Fox really was very bright for her tender years. Bel had bought Fox a stylish blue and grey pair of walking shoes in *Mountain Warehouse*, which were now safely ensconced in a box inside a paper carrier bag, swinging jauntily from Fox's hand.

"Where shall we go next?" Bel asked her

granddaughter.

"*Boots,* for make-up?" Fox suggested hopefully.

Bel and Maggie came down on the idea like two tons of bricks.

"Good heavens, no!"

"You're far too young for that, sweetheart!"

"And I don't know what your mummy would say either," Bel added. She really was genuinely unsure as to what Sophy would say. Was she a disciplinarian or an 'anything goes' type of parent? Who knows, thought Bel. Whichever she was, it seemed to work, as Fox was on the whole a very well-behaved, secure child.

"*I* know... how about the bookshop?" Maggie suggested cunningly. "Your granny tells me you got through quite a lot of that Jacqueline Wilson book last night!"

Bel felt a warm glow in her heart. She was still getting used to being called 'granny', and the pleasure had not diminished at all.

The town's main bookshop, when they found it, was a real gem, housed in the old Wool Exchange building. As they went inside the three of them gazed upward, open-mouthed with awe. It was built in a Gothic style, and had a vaulted roof like a church, together with arched windows and glittering leaded lights. Thick black beams on the plasterwork gave the place a Tudor feel. There were also wide staircases with an ornate, sweeping bannister, like something out of a fairytale castle, and the whole space was filled with bookcases crammed with colourful books. The women agreed that Fox could have ten pounds to spend, and look round on her own while they went upstairs for a hot drink. On the mezzanine floor you could sit in the balcony café with a coffee, cake and book, and admire the architecture below – and also keep an eye on your lively granddaughter if necessary. Maggie and Bel gasped at the four huge, round cakes on display - Hummingbird, Red Velvet, Guinness and Coffee and Walnut. Bel and Maggie each chose a coffee and a slice of cake, while Fox wandered around downstairs, seeking out her chosen books.

"So, how are things between you and Joe?" Bel asked, scooping a teaspoon of chocolate-sprinkled froth off the top of her cappuccino.

"What?" Maggie was taken aback by the question. What had Bel noticed? Had she somehow overheard that conversation they'd had about divorce? The thought filled Maggie with anxiety.

"Oh," Bel said casually, "I sensed there may be some kind of – atmosphere – between the two of you. Particularly that night at the *King's Head*. Correct me if I'm wrong, but there just seemed to be - I don't know - some kind of tension. It was all the more noticeable, as Joe's usually so chilled."

Maggie was unnerved at how perceptive her younger sister was. Well, maybe it was something to do with them having known eachother all their lives. But there was no way she wanted Bel to find out about Joe's divorce request. Not just now. Because that would make it seem more real, and Maggie wasn't ready to face that yet.

Maggie shovelled in another big forkful of red velvet cake. Comfort eating like this had become a habit of hers. Whenever unhappiness threatened, she would eat, craving that surge of joy and comfort. For her, eating a KitKat was like a hit of crack. Unfortunately, it was all beginning to take its toll on her body. These days, her voluminous linen trousers and flowing blouses were hiding an increasing amount of soft, roly flesh. Perhaps the eating was a sex substitute, she thought with a wry smile, as she and Joe weren't currently having any. Ah, dear. It was true that sometimes Maggie's life felt a little empty. Now she gazed down over the balcony at Fox, frolicking amongst the books and cushions. Maybe Maggie's own life would feel complete once she had a grandchild. But then, she knew she shouldn't rely on the advent of a grandchild to add meaning to her life. It would probably be an anti-climax anyway, she told herself, returning her to the mind-crushing boredom of young motherhood, only with the additional aches and pains of grandmotherhood thrown in!

"I don't know what you mean, Bel," she replied now, pretending to look puzzled. "I mean, perhaps Joe's been *slightly* subdued over the past few months, but I'd just put it down to some kind of midlife crisis.

As for things between me and him, they're absolutely fine."

Bel flicked a crumb off the skirt of her long, patterned tunic dress. "I mean, every marriage, or long-term relationship, is bound to go through its rough parts…"

Yes, and what would you know about it? Maggie thought indignantly, and was then ashamed at herself for having such a spiteful thought. She smiled warmly at her sister. "It's sweet of you to be concerned, Bel, but really, like I say, we're fine." Maggie drank down the last of her latte. Perhaps she should seek Joe out when they got back to the camp-site, have a word, knock this silly 'divorce' idea on the head once and for all. "Come on, Bel," she announced briskly, "let's head back now."

On the way back in the car, Fox said, "I might see Mummy this evening. Lucy said so." What? The two women turned to look at eachother - Bel raised an eyebrow at Maggie. Bel saw the need to proceed carefully. She'd had a little chat with Fox last night about how she was missing her mummy - "She texted me," Fox had sniffled, "and said she misses me too." Bel, still new to this game, had cuddled her close and reassured her as best she could.

"What exactly did Lucy say?" Bel asked gently, now, "About seeing your mummy?"

"She said she and Thomas want to go to the circus again, and if they did, they could take me and we could see Mummy. You could come too if you wanted,

Granny."

Bel couldn't deny the excitement that surged within her at the prospect of seeing Sophy. She herself was too proud to initiate the meet-up, but if the opportunity was handed to her on a plate, that'd be a different matter. But would she even be able to look her daughter in the eye, after she had treated her so shoddily over the years? "Hmm, well perhaps," she told Fox, patting her soft little hand. "We'll see."

*

There was no sign of his son when Joe and Rachael got back to the pod. Joe assumed that Thomas, and the others, were still deployed on their various outings. Briefly, he wondered how they were all getting on – Thomas, Lucy, Sebastian and Florence at the nature reserve – well Thomas would be in his element; he wasn't sure about the others - Maggie, Bel and Fox at the shopping centre in town. As for Barty, he'd been so arrogant and unhelpful earlier that Joe really didn't give a damn how he was getting on – Barty could've taken a running jump into the lake for all he cared.

Approaching it now, the pod seemed more inviting, less dark and gloomy than before. Joe was actually proud to unlock the front door and show it to Rachael. The way it was enclosed in its own little private garden, gathered in by hurdle fencing made of woven branches. The little garden having its own miniature area of decking, and a picnic table. Then there were the soft wooden panels of the interior, the curved triangular shape, the shaft of light pouring in from the single window at the top. It was almost church-like. The cosiness inside, the double airbed on the carpet, the patio doors letting in the leafy light. Joe hastily kicked the small amount of his and Thomas's detritus to one side.

Joe put the kettle on to boil and made Rachael a cup of tea. He opened the packet of luxury lemon and stem ginger cookies he'd bought for her. (He had popped to the camp shop earlier while he was waiting for her to come and pick him up in the car. Not wanting to tempt Fate but hoping against hope that she might come back with him later.)

They subsided onto the airbed, the tea forgotten for now.

"Sorry. I'm a little out of practise at seduction," Joe said, after kissing Rachael on the lips. (She had lovely lips - soft and full.) "I've only ever – with my w-" Before he could say the word that would definitely be a passion-killer, Rachael placed a finger on his lips, shushing him.

"You don't have to worry," she said, taking off his glasses, and setting them carefully down on the little shelf. "You're so attractive, and you don't even know it. It makes a change from all those cocky types."

When they kissed, Joe was suddenly reminded of the piercing in her tongue. It felt lovely; it gave a little something extra to the kiss. Perhaps he should get his done too, he thought, and then the bars would click against eachother, and tug on eachother... A mindblowing sensual sensation, he thought dreamily. And then he stopped thinking about anything for a while.

A bit later on he noticed that her tongue piercing was definitely noticeable for licking nipples and oral sex.

Afterwards, they cuddled up on the airbed and drank their now-cold tea. "Was that OK?" Joe asked anxiously. "I hope I didn't just rush you into that."

Rachael laughed. "You daft 'aporth. As if you could have rushed me into it; I felt very much in control of the process throughout. Anyway," she went on, quietly and matter-of-factly, "Sex is just sex, as long as it's consensual, bodies are just bodies and should be enjoyed." Then she blushed.

Joe was shocked at what he'd just done, and yet at the same time he couldn't help feeling elated. It occurred to him that he was playing with fire by bringing Rachael here, but he felt strangely reckless. Naïve soul that he was, he told himself that, at worst, it would be Thomas who discovered them, and that he, Joe, could pass it off as him 'just having a friend round for a cup of tea'... Wanting to see some daylight, Joe drew the curtains open and they gazed out at the greenery outside. Looking out from the pod, the curve of its eaves framed the pure blue sky and sun burnished trees.

"We could live like this," Joe said. "Stay right here

forever." Suddenly any lingering doubts about their relationship were gone, and he just felt that he and Rachael were exactly on the same page. He tried to put his thoughts into words. "I – I feel as if it's all I would need, you, the countryside, and a small, secure place like this to sleep."

Rachael grinned wryly. "It's certainly very, er, compact. But yes, I agree that being in the countryside is wonderfully soothing..."

Joe turned to her earnestly. "You've lived in quite a few unusual places, haven't you, Rach, like your boat, and that yurt in Wales. I - I could draw on your expertise. Try and be self-sufficient for energy, and grow my own food. I'm sick of the life I have now, working all day at Dotheboys Hall, with no room for relief or beauty in my life ..."

"Goodness," Rachael breathed. "I really like you too, Joe. But I have to admit, I'm feeling a little scared - like my feelings are running away from me." She turned to him. "I know I mustn't be reckless. I've been hurt by men before."

Joe stroked her hand. He was no fighter, but he thought he would like to beat up the men who had dared to hurt Rachael. He agreed that things were moving fast, but when you knew it was right, what was the point in wasting time? He for one wasn't getting any younger. He wished he'd met Rachael first! Sure, he and Maggie had loved eachother once. But they'd met too young, as idealistic student teachers from working class backgrounds, keen to 'better themselves'. They'd rushed to get married, thinking it was the thing to do – as it was, for many people, even as recently as the nineties. They hadn't had time to find out if they were truly compatible.

"It *does* sound amazing," Rachael went on, slowly, "your idea of living off-grid, in harmony with nature. I'd have to give up a few things, but I think life's about learning to let go. I'd be a bit sad to give up my counselling work, but I've got a friend I could pass my clients to. I'd also have to leave the café, and sell my boat, but I'd be prepared to do it."

Joe eyed her guiltily. "You'd give all that up - for me?"

"Not for *you*, exactly – " Rachael said. "But for our new way of life. You're right," she went on, slipping her arm through his, smiling up at him with those great dark eyes of hers. "We wouldn't need much, just good books, the odd board game, a real log fire, eachother. And maybe a cat. I've always wanted a cat."

Joe nodded eagerly. "You know, Rachael, I've been wondering whether I could buy a little cottage, somewhere pretty rural, where I could live off-grid. I was working out that, once the divorce came through, if I took some of my share of the house's value, yet still leave Maggie and the children comfortable, I would probably have about 30 grand…"

"30 grand? Wow, that's an impressive sum!"

"Yes well I suppose it *is* pretty impressive." Joe

frowned. "And I know I'm fortunate in that respect, and that I really shouldn't really moan. Some people would probably kill for a job like mine. And I've managed to save quite a lot. I *had* been hoping that'd be enough to buy the cottage." His expression darkened. "But I was chatting to one of the chaps I'm on holiday with, Barty, trying to gauge his expert opinion, and he said there was no way that would be enough money."

Rachael put her tea mug down. "Oh, that's a shame. Not even if you found somewhere really *really* run down and do it up? After all, they say, where there's a will there's a way…"

"Perhaps," said Joe thoughtfully. He really did want to make it happen. He suddenly thought of Barty's valuable watch, currently lying unworn and unheeded in the lodge. Barty is so rich, he said to himself – wealth he had inherited, not earned - that he probably wouldn't even notice if the watch was stolen. And yet that watch was worth £70,000. It could completely transform someone else's life. Like his – it could buy him that cottage in the Welsh wilds that he dreamed of.

Rachael peered out of the window. "Where are the rest of your family, anyway, and the other people you're on holiday with? It's like you're here, all on your own in this place."

Joe came back to reality with an unpleasant bump. "They went out, all of them." He glanced at his watch, a plain old, common-or-garden *Timex,* with a couple of scratches on the glass. "Actually I suppose they might be back quite soon."

"Oh, my God," Rachael said, straightening her clothing, smoothing down her bright mess of hair, yellow tangled in with the blue, scrambling to her feet. "Then I, my friend, shall be out of here." They kissed, passionately, one final time before parting.

No sooner had Rachael's 2CV sped off with a rattling of mud-guards, and the dust had had about five minutes to settle, than Maggie herself came marching up to his patio doors. Phew, that was a narrow squeak, Joe thought. He felt as if his heart had almost stopped, and the perspiration poured off him in buckets, as if he was in a tropical rainforest.

Joe hurried out to meet his wife on the decking. The last thing he wanted was for Maggie to go inside to his recently-vacated love nest, see the tangled sleeping bag, the two abandoned tea mugs. As he and Maggie came face to face, Joe felt like a right sleaze-bag; he felt sick with guilt over the fact that, just twenty or so minutes ago, he had been making love with Rachael.

Maggie tried to peer over his shoulder, into the pod. "Mm, this place looks pretty cosy," she said. "Better than I thought."

"Yes, it's growing on me," Joe said.

Maggie sniffed the air. "Can I smell perfume?" But it wasn't perfume, she decided. Not exactly. It was more like the fragrance of fresh flowers. Well, they were in the middle of the countryside.

Hastily, Joe steered Maggie towards the picnic bench. "Shall we sit here?" They both sat down, one each side of the table, beneath the shade of the umbrella.

Maggie ran her eyes over him, over his slightly crumpled outfit of checked shirt and beige shorts. "You're looking very boring," she said, frowning at his nondescript outfit. "Where's that nice red neckerchief I got you?"

"Oh, I, erm, think I must have lost it. Sadly." He blushed guiltily, recalling the sense of liberation he had felt when throwing the neckerchief out of the car window. At this very moment, it was probably blowing and fluttering freely and happily over the hills and hedgerows of Sussex. Maybe it had even provided a useful item of headgear for a sunburnt horse, he thought fancifully. He wondered if he was beginning to lose his marbles.

Maggie cleared her throat, indicating that the conversation was about to take a much more serious turn. "Did you really mean what you said the other day," she began, "about wanting a divorce?"

Joe steeled himself. "Well, yes, to be quite honest, I did." He tried to soften the blow. "We've had some great years together, Maggie, but – but I kind of feel our relationship has run its course. It's gone a bit stale."

Maggie frowned. "What, like some mouldy old loaf of bread?" She narrowed her eyes at him. "Joe, can I ask you something? Are you having some kind of midlife crisis?"

Joe bowed his head. He blushed. "To be honest, maybe. It's just everything – everything about my life seems wrong."

"Why didn't you talk to me?" Maggie asked, sounding hurt. "Tell me how you were feeling?"

"Oh, you know what it's like," Joe shrugged. "Life gets in the way, there's never any time. Y'know, we're always too busy working, shopping, cooking, doing chores. I used to love teaching," he went on. "I was so idealistic about it in the early days. I really wanted to make a difference. But now I'm completely ground down, the workloads are crazy. We're chronically understaffed. I just feel totally exhausted." He looked closely at her. "You're a teacher, too. Surely you get what I'm talking about?"

"Yes," Maggie replied, "but even after all these years I still feel passionate about my job! I love teaching English lit, and bringing it into the lives of each new generation of kids."

Joe looked at his wife in admiration. "You've always had more stamina than me, Mags."

"I suppose you could apply for early retirement," Maggie suggested, echoing what Barty had said earlier. "Or you could change career. Maybe you could go into tutoring, or work for Ofsted?"

Joe shook his head. "No; all I want is to get my own place, my own space, and do something completely different."

"We could get early retirement together," Maggie urged, desperation growing in her voice. "Travel the world, see some culture, all those things we always put off doing."

Joe shook his head. He felt agonised inside, as if he was killing something precious and defenceless, like a tiny bird. It was extremely strange to think of strong, feisty Maggie as a tiny bird. "I'm so sorry Maggie. But I just have to be on my own."

Maggie's expression darkened. "OK. I know I asked you before, but I'll ask you again, and I want you to be a hundred per cent honest with me – " her voice wavered slightly. "Is there another woman? Because I'm not stupid, Joe, I know there usually is in these cases."

Joe hesitated. Was he, was the male race really so predictable? The thought sickened him. Oh, God. This was the perfect time to tell her about Rachael, he knew. And yet he looked at his wife's unadorned, attractive face, her face that was usually so strong, and he could see unshed tears behind the hazel eyes, a definite quiver about the mouth. It frightened and pained him to see Maggie weakened and upset. Even though he knew it was stupid, and counter-intuitive of him, he did not want to be the source of her pain. "No, Maggie. I swear, there's no-one else."

Maggie smiled in relief. It was like the sun had come out from behind a cloud. "Well, that's something, at least." Nonsensically, Joe felt his own heart lifting too. "Joe, I have a favour to ask," she went on. "Do you think we could try to put on a united front, pretend, everything is normal between us, at least while the holiday lasts?" Joe felt horrified. This was an appalling idea. "I really want everyone to enjoy this time together – especially as it might be the last time we have together, ever."

Joe's heart quavered at her choice of words. He hesitated. "And then, after the holiday, we can talk seriously about divorce?"

Maggie nodded bravely. "If that's what you want, then I promise."

Joe sighed. He was weak, he was cowardly. He was in a hell of a mess. He knew that he was hurting both Rachael and, ultimately, Maggie. "OK, then," he said, with a heavy heart. God, everything was such a mess. When Maggie had gone, leaving him alone in the little garden, he put his head in his hands and sat like that for several minutes. The dark mood had descended again, and, even though the situation was of his own making, Joe was not sure how much more he could take. At that moment, he felt like just taking off, jacking it all in, and running away to live with Rachael, for good.

CHAPTER 6

Thomas felt tired but elated from his trip to the nature reserve. He must have walked several miles round its environs, in his attempt to identify as many items of flora and fauna as he possibly could. Florence had proved a charming, helpful companion, sometimes holding aside leaves or branches so he could get his photos. Thomas sighed. Really, after all that walking he'd have preferred to be relaxing on his lilo right now, reviewing the photos he'd taken. But he knew he had a window of opportunity between now and dinner-time, an opportunity he felt duty-bound to make the most of. So he headed off to the clubhouse, in pursuit of Barty.

The clubhouse was decorated in a luxurious, modern style, with mint-green, pale blue and sugared-almond pink armchairs and sofas gathered around low tables. All along one wall were big plate glass windows, giving a beautiful view of the sunset over the lake. Outside the pale blue sky was tinged with lemon on the horizon, as the sun started to sink lower, while the undersides of the clouds were illuminated with gold. Everything, including inside the clubhouse, was bathed in light; it was the golden hour. Even Barty looked quite handsome, Thomas thought dispassionately, sitting alone at a table nursing a glass of whisky, his hawk-like nose ennobled with gilded highlights, even his tousled auburn curls looking like they had been carved by some sculptor. Normally he had great trouble seeing what his sister saw in the man. Barty was wearing his 'casual smart' gear for the pub, a navy blue V neck jumper over a white Viyella shirt, and stone coloured trousers. Thomas approached him with some apprehension; he almost felt as if he was anxiously twisting a metaphorical cap in his hands, or possibly tugging at his non-existent forelock.

*

Perfect, Barty thought. Solitude, an alcoholic drink, a good book – even if this one was proving slightly heavy-going, nothing was worth doing unless it was a bit of a challenge. Ensconced in his throne-like armchair, he felt large, majestic. This feeling was habitual for him. When he sat on a chair, he dominated it, it felt tiny under his stature. And when you were of his build, tall, muscular – OK, slightly overweight – it was hard not to stride. Everything he did was along extravagant lines. He loved to eat, to drink. To savour an exquisite meal or a fine wine or cognac. Coming from an affluent background, luxurious food and drink had never been in short supply for him. He was born to it, entitled to it; so why not do it? Sighing pleasurably, he took another mouthful of whisky, and turned another page of his book.

*

It had been Lucy's idea for Thomas to curry favour with Barty. "You hate your job, don't you?" she'd asked him, walking him back to his pod after their outing.

"Well, duh, it's picking litter off a conveyor belt. What's there to love?"

Lucy raised her eyebrows. "I don't know, you could say it's a worthy cause, aiding the recycling process?"

"It is, I know, but it's also mindless and monotonous. And poorly paid."

"OK," she nodded. "In which case, why don't you try sweet-talking Barty, see if he'd be prepared to give you a job on the magazine?" She silenced Thomas's protests. "I know, I know, you haven't always found him the easiest to get on with, and you're kind of on opposite sides of the political spectrum. But I promise you, his bark is far worse than his bite. Deep down, he's really just a pussy cat..."

With these confusing, animal-based mixed metaphors in his mind now, Thomas pushed the door of the clubhouse open. Across the room, he surveyed his quarry. Thomas made his way nervously amongst the scattering of guests, up to Barty's table – the other man had not noticed him yet. He was engrossed in his whisky, and the expensively-leather-bound volume he was reading.

Coming to a standstill at his table, Thomas cleared his throat. "What's that you're reading?" and Barty jumped out of his skin, almost as if he'd been caught doing something he shouldn't.

"Oh, Thomas, old chap, it's you!" he said, sounding relieved. "This old thing? It's an anthology of the Metaphysical Poets. Come, sit down, have a drink!" Imperiously, Barty waved a barman over, though it was meant to be service at the bar only.

Thomas joined Barty in a whisky. He didn't like the taste very much, but he thought it would be a friendly thing to do. But what the hell could he talk to Barty about? They had nothing in common. Any attempts to converse would seem so fake. And was it really Thomas's vibe to go grovelling like this, anyway? He kind of hated himself for it.

Then Thomas noticed the watch, the watch that was worth a bloody fortune. The – what was it called? Patek Philippe, with its pale golden face and tan leather strap, nestling securely on Barty's arm below an immaculate white shirt cuff and an inch or so of cushiony freckled skin.

"That really is a very fine watch, Barty," Thomas commented, pointing at it.

"Isn't it just?" Barty's face flushed pink with pleasure, glancing down at the aforementioned item. "These things are pricy for good reason. Quality, handwork, heritage and the use of precious metals and stones such as gold, platinum and diamond..." And then he proceeded to talk about the finer points of that particular watch, and of the many other valuable watches he had in his collection. Meanwhile Thomas stifled a yawn.

*

The reunited party had dinner together in the lodge that night, vegan curry cooked by Seb and Florence. Lucy had got Seb to stop off at a flower shop on the drive back from the nature reserve, and, as promised, she'd bought a lovely bouquet for Fox. Before the evening meal was served, Fox went round distributing flowers to everyone in the lodge - she put white Chrysanthemums in Lucy's and Florence's hair; dark red Gerbera in Maggie and Bel's hair, and purple and pink-tinged chrysanthemums in the four men's buttonholes. The remaining flowers went in an old pasta sauce jar filled with water, where they looked surprisingly elegant.

Then just as Lucy was going to take her place at the dinner table, Bel waylaid her, saying in a low voice, "I hear you and Thomas are going to the circus again tonight, and hoping to take Fox, too." Lucy had expected Bel to be upset by this fact, so was surprised when she went on, "Actually, Lucy, sweetheart, I think I might come too, if that's OK."

"Of course, that's fine, Aunty Bel," Lucy murmured. "I expect you know we're intending to meet up with Sophy afterwards. I'm sure she'll be thrilled to see you." Lucy felt the need to reassure her aunt, aware as she was of how rocky relations between her and her daughter had been for a while now. She loved her aunty, but she had to bite her tongue to avoid voicing her true opinion – that surely, in any falling-out, the onus was always on the parent to build bridges?

Bel's stiff upper lip had been trembling throughout their conversation, up to the point where she finally dissolved into tears as she admitted, "Really? You think she'd agree to see me? Oh, I'd love to see my Sophy, my baby! I've missed her so much. You see, Lucy, I – I fear I may have misjudged her." And Lucy, who had a soft heart under her feisty exterior, gave her aunt a quick, fierce hug.

All this was well and good, even pretty heartwarming. Then they all sat down to dinner, and were enjoying the curry, when, to make conversation Lucy mentioned the planned trip to the circus. Seb was sitting right across the table from her, and she was purposely avoiding his eye. If she looked at him, she would remember the kiss they'd shared in the hide, and the thought made her feel sick with guilt. Her own behaviour had surprised her - she'd thought she was pretty respectable these days, but it seemed her wild streak was as wild as ever. She'd acted in the heat of the moment, following an impulse that had seemed impossible to resist, but with hindsight she could see how wrong it had been. He was Barty's son, for fuck's sake! In the aftermath of the event, Lucy had firmly reminded herself that Barty was her partner, *he* was the man she loved, which meant that from now on she must remain cool and level-headed towards Sebastian at all times, and make sure there was no opportunity for them to be alone together. It was simply best not to put herself in that situation. Well Lucy would have to have been made of stone not to be susceptible to those looks, and that charm. (Lucy couldn't help but think that Barty's first wife must have been a total femme fatale, to have donated those genes to Sebastian. A sneaky look on Facebook had only served to confirm this suspicion, and tug at Lucy's insecurities.)

However, now Seb laid down his knife and fork, pushed his half-eaten poppadum aside and said, "Actually, guys, Florence and I would like to join the circus expedition too, if that's OK." He smiled round the table, his eyes finally coming to rest on Lucy, meeting her gaze boldly. Lucy felt her whole body flush with heat. She felt intensely uncomfortable, wishing she could leave the table there and then.

Instead, she picked up her glass and gulped down half a pint of water. But she gulped it too quickly, and then started to choke a little bit. "Are you all right, Lucy?" her mother asked, concerned, reaching up to pat her on the back. Apart from this sudden flurry of attention, both of her parents had been very quiet during the meal, as if they were preoccupied with something, too.

"Yes, I'm fine," Lucy reassured her quickly. "The curry was a bit hot, that's all."

"Do we take it that's a 'yes' then?" Florence asked,

smiling amenably.

"Oh yes, of course," Thomas said gallantly. "It would be lovely to have you both along for the evening! The more the merrier!" The party was growing by the minute. Now there would only be Maggie, Joe and Barty remaining at home. If Thomas was disappointed at all at the additions to their outing, he made a very good job of not showing it. Well, he was a pretty amenable chap on the whole.

Lucy also nodded her agreement. Well, there was no way she and Thomas could say 'no' to Seb and Florence joining them, especially when they'd cooked such a delicious meal.

*

After dinner, those who were going to the circus went off to get ready. Lucy felt rather apprehensive as she got changed and did her make-up. It didn't help that she was wearing her bra and knickers to do her make-up, so as not to get any make-up on her outfit, and Barty kept casting her appreciative glances across the bedroom, from where he was supposed to be working on his *magnum opus*. They had reconciled some of their differences since she'd got back from the trip. Because she felt guilty about the kiss with Sebastian, Lucy had softened her stance slightly towards Barty, telling him that she might, after all, be prepared to leave the holiday early, if the interview with *Hello* magazine meant so much to him.

Barty had been delighted about this, and said that,

yes, the interview would go down *so* much better if she featured in it, too. Stifling the familiar feeling that she was just eye candy to him, an accessory to his career, Lucy reminded herself of what a terrible thing she'd done that afternoon, and forced herself to keep her lip buttoned.

Now Barty approached across the bedroom, gently lifted up her hair, and kissed the nape of her neck. In spite of everything, she felt herself quiver with pleasure. But romantic advances from Barty were the last thing she needed right then – she needed to keep her mind firmly on the agenda for that night's trip to the circus, as it was now potentially fraught with danger and sexual tension. She turned round and smiled at Barty, then kissed him chastely, dismissively on the lips. Hastily, she got up, reached for her dress and slipped it on, managing to zip the back up without asking him for help.

*

Sophy was super-excited for that night's show, mainly because her daughter was coming to watch, and she would get to see her afterwards. She had bought Fox a special cuddly narwhal to take back to the holiday place with her. It was lovely, soft blue plush with a pearly rainbow tusk - Sophy was just a big kid at heart, and had half wanted to keep it for herself.

At least she was keeping herself busy, so the time went quicker - she was filming a video for TikTok – 'a Day in the life of a circus performer'. If Fox had been with her 24/7, Sophy knew she wouldn't even have been able to consider doing something like this. In the long term she was hoping to build some kind of online presence, which might even lead to a new, additional income source, you never knew.

Despite the fact that she was missing her daughter terribly, life seemed good at the moment. Sophy had been seeing someone at the circus for a few weeks now – a ridiculously-toned, good-looking acrobat called Rafael – and while her daughter was away, Sophy had temporarily moved into Raf's place. It was lovely to be together all the time and just do their training and chill. Her true character could come out, without the strain of being a mum for once. During the day she and Raf both walked round half-naked in their caravan, clad only in their underwear in the summer heat, entirely comfortable with their bodies which were muscular and spare. After all, their bodies were what they worked on all the time, they were essential to their careers. Sophy would pause during her training to scamper over and plant a kiss on Raf's lips while he was doing his stretches; Raf's pecs brushed Sophy's bare shoulders as he slipped behind her while she was making the lunch in the little kitchen. Chicken breasts, avocado and cherry tomatoes, with a little sprinkling of magic, chipotle vinaigrette. On a daily basis, she had to steel herself to resist Rafael, not to turn round and fall into his arms. Otherwise she'd never get anything done! Temptation was always a whisker away. The space in his caravan was so confined, they were bound to always be brushing up against eachother; the two of them were still in their honeymoon period, and the electricity between them was palpable.

"I'm so looking forward to see my little Foxie," she'd told him the previous day, almost dancing with excitement. "Although it's been a relief to have a break, and spend some proper time with you, I do miss her so much, the little sprout." In fact it was like a physical pain inside her.

"I know you miss her, my darling, it's only natural." Raf's face fell slightly as he regarded Sophy. "But it's also been really nice being just the two of us, babe."

"I know," she agreed, sighing. "And I suppose I'll have to go back to my own place after the show tonight, so I can meet the relatives there. I don't feel quite ready to tell them about you yet, my sweet boy. I feel there's enough upheaval at the moment as it is." It was the first time Sophy had had a serious relationship since Fox's father. Oh dear, she was not sure what the answer to life's conundrum was. She often felt as though she was being pulled in two – or maybe even three – directions. Could there be some kind of workable solution, where Fox spent half her time at the circus, and half her time with relatives? Maybe, though Sophy wasn't sure her mother deserved to play a bigger role in her granddaughter's life, seeing as she had showed so little interest up to this point. Really, Sophy reckoned she had come off pretty poorly in the 'parental' stakes – there was the situation with her mum, and as for her dad, she'd never had any contact with him since he'd left home when she was five. In fact, the only family she'd ever really had was the circus.

It had taken Sophy a little while to trust Raf, purely because she wasn't used to trusting people. But they worked together on the trapeze, and in their act at least, trust was essential. Raf seemed like one of the good ones outside of the big top, too, and as well as being generally supportive he'd agreed to help her film the video. They watched it back together now (what he'd filmed so far). The opening scene showed her cheekily giving him one final cuddle in bed, then getting up in the little caravan bedroom – whose small dimensions appeared even smaller due to the amount of fitted, dark furniture in it. After a protein-rich breakfast of avocado on toast, fried eggs and bacon, it was time for Training, which she and Raf did together in the Big Top. Clad in athletics shorts and a cropped vest top, her flame-coloured hair pulled back in a ponytail, Sophy trained on the gymnastics rings. Gripping onto the rings, she swung her legs up into the air, high above her head. Her legs were solid, muscular. Upside down, she did the splits in the air. Pointed both her legs to one side and then the other. It would all look graceful and effortless in the show, but for now it was sweaty, grunting hard work and endurance. Finally, Sophy swung her legs back down to earth. Her finishing pose, arms thrust upwards, segued naturally into some dancing, strutting, rolling movements. She was proud of her work on the rings, she felt like showing off. A lot of performing was about the confidence, the swagger. She met Raf's eye while he was doing some push-ups and he grinned at her. Feeling the familiar flame of sexual attraction flare within her, she grinned back.

After training it was Lunch, then time to chill for a bit, after which the evening routine began. This included preparing dinner for after the show, and then putting on her make-up – Sophy filmed herself covering blemishes, then painting on a big red cupid's bow, and exaggerated black wings curving upwards from the corners of her eyes. Like the outfit, which was glitzy, sparkly crystals on a pink and purple dress with flesh coloured parts making it seem more revealing than it actually was, the make-up was cleverly deceptive, intended to be seen from a distance. Everything here was exaggerated, larger than life. It made ordinary life seem very dull. Sophy wondered if her little Fox was finding that to be the case, while she was staying with her grandmother in the mundane, ordinary world.

Sophy checked her appearance in the mirror. When she thought about her own mother, she didn't feel much emotion. She was OK with Fox staying with Bel, (and the others,) as long as *she* personally didn't have to interact with her too much. After all, Mum had been so contemptuous, so dismissive of the life Sophy had chosen, that Sophy had shut all thoughts of her away in a mental compartment which she didn't have to visit very often, to spare herself from the hurt. Because it *was* hurtful. Surely if her mother knew Sophy loved something, was talented and committed to it, she should respect that out of love for her daughter?

When she stepped out of the caravan, the sun was sinking towards the horizon, the countryside bathed in a golden glow. Excitement growing within her now, Sophy walked with Raf towards the big top. Soon they were swallowed up by the tent, the pumping music, the whoops of the crowd. Suddenly Sophy spotted Fox in the crowd, and her heart contracted. They waved frantically to eachother, and Sophy was worried she might cry. She gritted her teeth, held it together, stayed focused.

Once things got underway, she entered a different world, addicted to the drug of performing. When it was her act, Sophy shinned up the ladder. Adrenaline coursed through her; she took a deep breath, then jumped from the high platform, catching on to her trapeze. She flew through the air, swooping up close to people's faces, or so it felt, things getting huge then small again. She swung closer to her daughter in the audience, and felt as if she was almost able to reach out and touch her. Sophy hung from the trapeze by her hands, turned a somersault, then caught back on to the trapeze with her legs. She sat on the trapeze as if it was a playground swing, then caught onto Raf's hands – hanging upside down, he swung her, looped her round before she leapt away, catching back on to her own trapeze. She landed back on the platform with a sharp intake of breath that it had gone OK, then did her finishing pose, bold, arms thrust upwards, to rapturous applause from the crowd.

Sitting in the audience, Bel watched her daughter perform, a joyous expression on her face. She did not fear for her daughter, for she was a creature not quite of this world; she was a fairy; a flying sprite. Bel bit her lip, then glanced across at Fox. "Isn't Mummy clever?" she whispered to the little girl. "Isn't she amazing? I'm *so* proud of her."

Fox nodded, grinning broadly, her smile all teeth. A tear trickled down Bel's cheek, the pleasure of watching her daughter bittersweet.

Sitting on the other side of Fox, Lucy also gazed upwards, rigid with concentration. She watched her cousin with her heart in her mouth, totally mesmerised. Once again, Lucy was consumed by the transforming magic of the circus. The vastness, the darkness, the lights and the colour. Lucy glanced down the row of seats, first to the left, then to the right. Bel and Fox looked blissfully happy; Thomas and Florence looked enthralled. Everyone was still adorned with the flowers Fox had given them earlier. How Lucy had come to be sitting between Seb and Fox, she was not entirely sure. She watched Sophy land safely on the platform at the end of her act, felt a surge of relief, and then suddenly felt Seb's hand reach out and squeeze her own. Lucy's cheeks felt flushed, warm, her eyes moist. She turned towards Seb; their eyes met, and then Lucy relented and returned his smile. Her earlier resolutions had crumbled into dust; life was too short not to lay yourself open to joy wherever you found it. She squeezed Seb's hand back.

*

After the show, most of them trotted over to the little red and white caravan. The thrill of the circus still hung over them, and Bel and Fox were hand in hand, both of them happy and starry-eyed. The group were greeted at the caravan door by Sophy. After the initial greetings, and an emotional hug between Sophy and Fox, Fox scampered off to her bedroom to reacquaint herself with her favourite possessions. In the absence of the little girl's uniting presence, Sophy and Bel stood face to face in the small sitting-room, neither smiling, both reluctant to meet the other's eye. Then suddenly Bel blurted out, "I'm so sorry, Sophy, my darling. I've been a pretty rubbish mother over the last few years. Will you forgive me?"

Sophy hesitated for a moment. Then she sighed, then calmly opened her arms, allowing Bel to step inside them, and she closed her arms around her, patting her on the back, comforting the sobbing Bel as if she was a small child. All the while, Sophy said nothing.

"I'll make it up to you," Bel said. "If you'll let me – I promise."

Finally, Sophy spoke. She stepped back from her

mother, regarding her seriously. "It'll take time," she said, her voice wavering on the verge of tears. "For me to let you back in, Mum. It - it's not going to happen overnight."

"I know," said Bel. "I understand. I've got all the time in the world."

Thomas couldn't help feeling touched, as he observed this scene from the sidelines – although he did think Bel was laying it on slightly thick. He shifted awkwardly on his feet, feeling a bit like a third wheel – he had been planning to tell Lucy about his chat in the clubhouse with Barty as soon as he got the opportunity, but she seemed to have disappeared off somewhere, he knew not where. It was rather embarrassing, as Florence was also standing around in Sophy's caravan – if Thomas was the third wheel then she must be the fourth - having been temporarily abandoned by Sebastian.

*

Outside, it was rapidly getting dark. Lucy and Sebastian had slipped away from the others as they left the circus tent, with Sebastian making straight for the souvenir stand, where he queued up with the little kiddies and bought a handful of glow sticks, of which he gave half to Lucy. Laughing, Seb joined two or three together to make a circle, and placed it on Lucy's head, like a luminous rainbow crown, which cast an unearthly light over her pretty face. She used her share of the glow sticks to make a necklace, which she placed around his neck. Giggling, they wandered off across the field, hand in hand, floating, luminous blobs of colour tracking their route in the dimness. Pausing to think for a moment, it occurred to Lucy to wonder what the hell she was playing at. But she felt oddly reckless, and dismissed the thought. Gradually they got further and further from the crowd.

"Bet you're glad to get away from Dad for the evening," Seb teased her. "That man can be such a bore at times."

Lucy made an attempt to look prim and proper. "Believe it or not, I do actually enjoy his company," she replied, before feeling compelled to add, "at times. And besides," she went on, feeling the desire to push Seb's buttons, "if *he's* a bore, then you're a spoilt, ungrateful, public school brat!" Sometimes she just wanted to let rip at Sebastian, as she sensed he could take it, and give back as good as he got.

"Oho, really? Well, my God, Lucy, it's several years since I've been at public school. I'm a big boy now."

She raised an eyebrow. "So you say."

Seb's eyes were sparkling, his expression was confident. "Come on, seriously, I know you can't really prefer him to me."

"Sebastian, you're just frustrated, because you can't have your own way for once."

"What do you mean?" he challenged.

"Well, it's clear you've always used your looks to

get what you want."

Sebastian's face broke into a broad smile, that made dimples appear in his cheeks, and accentuated the square cut of his chin. "Ah, so you admit you think I'm attractive?"

"Well of course you bloody are," Lucy said, thinking, is he for real?

Then, suddenly Sebastian froze, drawing Lucy close beside him. "Look!" he whispered, pointing, as the pale, ghost-like silhouette of an owl glided through the twilight. "I expect you know, but it's a barn owl," he went on. "This is the time of day they like to search for prey." The owl disappeared into the trees at the edge of the field.

"Wow," Lucy breathed. She turned to Seb. Suddenly the frivolity of a few moments ago had vanished. "Seriously, I love that you care so much about nature, and the environment. I've decided, I definitely want to get into environmental activism."

"Great. You'll have to join us on a protest sometime."

"I'd like that," Lucy smiled. "I want to have a break from writing articles about climate change, and so on, to actually trying to *do* something about it." Her mouth twisted. Barty probably wouldn't approve; he would think it was a whole lot of fuss about nothing. But then it wasn't up to him, was it?

"There's bats around, too," Sebastian said, gazing

upward. "If you look closely, you can see them darting around."

"Oh, wow, yes. Gosh," Lucy squealed. "Oh dear. I know it's bad, but they slightly creep me out! Those weird little faces, and I'm worried their wings will brush my face!" She cringed against Sebastian, and he laughed, slipping his arm around her waist and pulling her closer, in a way that made her heart beat faster.

"Don't worry," he said. "They're not going to bother you. What they're looking for is moths and insects. They're pipistrelles," he went on. "Cute little things. They won't eat you up, but I might," he drawled, jokingly. Suddenly he pressed his warm, open mouth to the side of her neck, and bit very gently.

Lucy felt tingles all up and down her body. It took every ounce of her willpower to be serious, and say, "No, Seb, don't. You mustn't."

"Mustn't I? What a shame. I've been wanting to get you on your own all evening. That kiss at the hide earlier was something else."

Lucy blushed, glad that he could not see this in the growing darkness. She thought again about Florence, whom Sebastian had assured her was just a friend'. She wasn't sure whether she believed him or not. Seb's blue eyes were hard to read. Was he sincere, or was he stringing her along, telling her what she wanted to hear so that he could seduce her? It did not help that his eyes always held a kind of ironic expression, dancing with mischief. They stood there at the edge of the field, and gazed searchingly at eachother. His arms were around her waist in the thin summery dress, and she placed her hands on his shoulders.

"I know this is crazy," Seb said suddenly, "seeing as we've only just met. But the thing is, Lucy, I think I love you."

This declaration should have come as a huge, thrilling shock to her, but the thing was, Lucy felt as if she already knew it. It was as if it had always been written in the stars that they should be together. "I – I know," she heard herself agreeing, infected with the magic of the night. "I feel as if I love you too. I - I've never met anyone like you. If only we could be together," she went on miserably, "but we can't. I'm with your father."

His eyes scanned her face in the gloom as if trying to read her expression. Her face beneath the glowing rainbow crown, he thought to himself - there was something supernatural about her; she looked more like a pagan goddess than ever. Then he kissed her, the kiss became passionate, and suddenly they were lying in the grass, fumbling at eachother's clothes.

Lucy's feeling of recklessness increased. Suddenly she just wanted him inside her, and she raised herself to him, pushing his hips, pushing him down into her. His dark curly hair hung down around his face as he gazed down at her. Sweat dampened his curls, and glistened on his forehead. He looked so beautiful she could hardly breathe. He seemed almost bemused by her eagerness. "Are you - protected?" he whispered.

"Yes," she replied recklessly, knowing there was no chance she could get pregnant. She raised her mouth demandingly to his, devouring him in a kiss.

CHAPTER 7

Some time later, after they had straightened their clothes, they walked back towards the circus, hand in hand, Lucy feeling ecstatic. She had just made love to a gorgeous man who she was newly in love with. Surely the opportunities for such things did not come round very often. Sebastian aroused feelings in her that Barty never had – both emotionally and physically. She decided to enjoy the post-coital high, to just live in the moment, but knowing that the guilt would follow later. The crowds had disappeared now. There was only the odd circus employee wandering around, clearing things up for the night. Then suddenly they saw a familiar figure striding across the grass towards them, a big scowl on his face, like a big, angry bear. Very much living up to his namesake, Lucy thought, observing in horror that it was Barty.

"Where the hell have you two been?" he demanded, when he caught up to them. "And what the hell have you got on your head, Lucy? It's wonky, whatever it is!" Lucy raised a hand to straighten her glow stick crown. Somewhere in the throes of passion she had lost Fox's white chrysanthemum, but the glowing crown was very much still there, albeit askew. Barty's face was angry and red. The others –

Bel, Fox, Thomas and Florence – could be seen trailing along in his wake. Fox was clutching a large, cuddly narwhal, as if it was some kind of life buoy.

"We – we weren't expecting you to come and get us, Bear," Lucy stuttered. "We were planning on getting an Uber back."

"Well I decided to come and get *you*. I thought you'd be grateful!"

"Dad," Sebastian drawled, "stop behaving like an utter twat."

Thomas privately agreed with this sentiment, though he said nothing. Barty could be a right grumpy old shit at times. Just because Lucy and Seb had wandered off for a walk together. (Thomas could be a bit of an innocent at times, believing the best of people, not always reading the deeper meanings.) Everyone was subdued as they all trooped back to Barty's car, the happy mood of the evening gone. Thomas felt sorry for Lucy, having to live with a man whose mood could turn so suddenly. Thomas had to ask himself the question, Was this man even right for his sister?

*

That night, just before bed, Lucy was just coming out of the bathroom as Sebastian was heading for it. They exchanged a longing look, and then he blew her a kiss just before she disappeared into her bedroom. Lucy slipped into bed next to a snoring Barty, her heart pounding rapidly. She felt as if her body was still tinging from the forbidden sex; she even fancied she could still smell Sebastian on her. But she had washed thoroughly so it must be her overactive imagination.

Because of the heat, the bedroom window was open quite wide, and she could hear the sound of the fountain, which splashed all night long. Lucy lay there for over an hour before sleep finally claimed her. During that time, just as she'd predicted – and deserved – her blissful happiness started to drain away, leaving her with the guilt and the self-recriminations. She had done a terrible thing – not only had she had unprotected sex, which was risky in itself even though she knew she couldn't get pregnant. But she had been unfaithful to Barty, and with a man who was himself not even free to be with her. She could barely bring herself to think about what she'd done, and the fact that two innocent parties had potentially been hurt by her actions.

*

The following morning, all hell broke loose. Barty was angry – and it was not because he'd discovered Lucy's unfaithfulness, for that was still unbeknownst to him. "Where the hell's my watch?" Barty boomed, flinging open his bedroom door. He'd been in the process of getting dressed after his shower and was currently wearing shorts and a bathrobe. "The Patek Philippe?"

The other inhabitants of the lodge, who'd been in the middle of breakfast or getting dressed, stopped what they were doing and started looking for the watch. They looked under cushions, inside drawers and behind cereal boxes, but there was no sign of it.

"Can you remember where you last had it?" Maggie asked Barty sensibly.

"God, I knew someone was going to ask me that bloody question!" he thundered. Everyone was starting to see another side to the blundering, affable Barty. At least Maggie was used to dealing with difficult secondary school pupils, so she didn't quail. "And *fortunately*," Barty ranted on, "I can give a very precise answer – it was on my dressing-table, right next to my *Thomas Ford* aftershave!"

Lucy took a deep breath and counted to ten. "Barty, my love, please try to calm down," she said. "I'm sure it'll turn up in a minute. And besides," she went on, "you've got it insured, haven't you?"

"Well yes of course I have, but that's hardly the point. That watch has sentimental value - as far as I'm concerned, it's irreplaceable!"

Thomas could hear the stressed, raised voices filtering through the trees as he approached the lodge. He was already feeling anxious, concerned that his dad hadn't come home to the pod the previous night. Maybe him and Mum had ended up getting romantic and he had spent the night at the lodge, he wondered? It was a gross thought, but it would still be a relief. Waking earlier than usual, he'd decided to get dressed and wander over to the lodge, although now he was beginning to wish he hadn't, instinctively shying away from the raised voices he could hear. He had to quell an instinct to flee, back to the safety and quiet of the pod.

Tentatively, he opened the door and stuck his head in.

"Aha!" Barty exclaimed, instantly pouncing on him. "Just the chap I wanted to see. My Patek Philippe has gone missing, and I seem to recall that you were taking quite an interest in it in the club house yesterday evening!"

Thomas's cheeks flooded with heat. "So what are you saying, that I've *stolen* it?"

Barty's bushy brows drew together in a frown. "You have to admit, it looks a bit suspicious, doesn't it?"

Lucy went up to Barty and put her hand on his arm. "Bart, you can't just accuse him. You haven't got any evidence, nor any real reason to think he's taken it."

"Well he was asking me loads of questions about the watch last night, and besides, everyone knows how stony broke he is!"

"Barty! Don't be so horrible," Lucy protested. "That's my brother you're talking about."

"Yes, come on, that's hardly fair to Thomas," Florence chipped in.

Meanwhile Bel cuddled Fox close, trying to shield

her from all the unpleasantness.

"I was only showing an interest to be polite, you fucking pompous old git," Thomas shot back angrily, as Bel hastily led Fox into their bedroom.

Maggie stepped forward. "Of course Thomas hasn't taken it – I'm sure that if we just keep looking, we'll find it," she said soothingly, though her face looked doubtful. "Thomas, sweetie, where is your dad? Is he up yet?"

"No," Thomas said distractedly. "He didn't come back to the pod last night. I was coming over to see if he'd stayed the night here."

Maggie shook her head. "No, darling, I haven't seen him since after dinner last night." Her face fell. "I assumed he'd spent the evening in the pod." Her conversation with her husband about divorce was still uppermost in her mind. She'd felt it had gone OK, all things considered - Maggie hadn't got exactly what she wanted out of it, an end to the talk of divorce, but she felt she'd at least secured a stay of execution. And with time she'd hoped she could change his mind about it. But now Joe was missing and she wasn't so sure. Surely he hadn't just gone off and left her like that – abandoned their marriage in a sudden, dramatic gesture? The thought filled her with panic and nausea. Oh God, everything seemed to be going wrong. This was supposed to be the perfect holiday, the chance to repair everything that was wrong with their family.

"Anyway, never mind that!" Barty snapped. "What about my bloody watch? Someone here," he glared at Thomas, "knows exactly where it is."

Thomas scowled. "I'm going to check if Dad's arrived back at the pod." And he turned and stormed off out of the lodge, banging his angrily way down the metal steps.

*

Meanwhile, nine miles away in the town of Haughton, Joe was shocked at himself. Well, he'd well and truly gone and done it now. He'd known he had to get away, that there was no way he could stay at the lakeside park any longer.

At first when he'd woken up the day after it all happened, he wasn't quite sure where he was. He turned his head on the pillow, surprised to find he was lying in a proper bed rather than a Lilo. Then it all started to come painfully back to him. It had started the previous night, with him once again sunk in gloom, feeling as if he was drowning in a swirling mixture of desperation and frustration. Desperation that he seemed trapped in this loveless charade with Maggie, and frustration that, due to his financial situation, it would never be possible for him to be with the woman he loved. In the end, he had resolved to take drastic action. It seemed as though Barty's watch was the answer to his prayers, a convenient source of the extra money he so desperately needed to buy his off-grid cottage. And Barty probably wouldn't even notice it was gone. It was time to be bold, be daring! After all, where had being timid and sensible got him all his life? (OK, they had got him a loving family, a decent house and a headmastership, but these were not the focus of his thoughts just then.)

As soon as people had departed for the circus, Maggie had gone for a lie-down and Barty was in the shitter, Joe had crept into Lucy and Barty's room, moving swiftly over to the dressing-table, and snatching up Barty's valuable watch before he could think twice about it. Then, the watch secreted in his pocket, he had quickly departed the lodge and made his way back to the glamping pod. There he'd changed into his new outfit, the black jeans, suede boots and jacket – a new look for a new life. He'd packed a few things, including his sleeping bag, and left the holiday park. The Patek Philippe was now safely stowed in a zipped compartment of his rucksack. Joe didn't take the Rover as he wanted Maggie and the kids to have use of it – they deserved it; he did not. He'd set off, walking along the edge of the winding country road that led from the holiday park, his thumb stuck out for a lift. It was starting to get dark and the roads were pretty quiet. Finally a driver had taken pity on him, and given Joe a ride into town.

For a while after he'd been dropped off, he had trudged through the night-time streets of the town, desperately trying to find a place to sleep. He couldn't go straight to Rachael – he had to warn her first of what he'd done – and besides, he didn't even know her home address. His first port of call had been McDonalds, a place he didn't usually visit, but it looked cheerful and the prices were cheap. He ordered a McPlant burger, fries and a large diet Coke, and was surprised by how tasty it was. There was also a socket to recharge his phone, and the staff didn't seem to be hassling people to move on - perhaps he would even stay there all night, he thought, as it was one of those 24 hours ones. The later it got, however, the more the quality of the clientele deteriorated, and people were starting to get a bit loud and lairy, when a muscular man with tattoos had approached him.

"I saw you just then, looking at me funny," the man accused him.

"No," Joe said. "I didn't."

"Are you calling me a liar?" The man drew himself up to his full six foot four or so, looking as if he was very much ready for a fight.

Feeling as if his life had started to get a bit surreal, and physically exhausted, Joe had squared up to the man, even attempting to throw a punch at him when the man repeated his accusation. Fortunately the punch missed, and at that moment a policewoman had appeared and suggested Joe might like to leave the premises. And so Joe made his way out of the town heading for a more residential area, supposing that he would doss down in someone's back garden, behind a bush or a large shrub – at least the weather was still pretty mild, even at night. Then he'd spotted in someone's back garden a convenient shed – a shed which, upon turning its door handle, appeared not to be locked and which, upon stepping inside, had turned out to be quite a comfortably furnished 'Man Cave'. Or perhaps more accurately, to judge by the nature of the furnishings, a 'Woman Cave'. Joe couldn't quite believe his luck. He certainly didn't deserve such good fortune. The good-sized shed contained a single bed, a small bistro style patio table and two chairs, and lots of twee, nautical-themed wall-hangings and knick-knacks. He'd crawled under the blue-checked blankets and throws on the single bed, and fallen straight to sleep, until the morning sunlight pouring in through the windows had woken him.

Shit, thought Joe now, shielding his eyes from the light, I'd better get out of here before the owner discovers me. He scrambled out of bed just as his phone made a bleeping noise. It was a text from Maggie. The subject matter of the text made his blood run cold. *'Joe, where are you? I'm worried about you, and Barty's expensive watch has gone missing and he's accusing Thomas of having stolen it.'* Maggie's texts were always quite wordy. No abbreviations or emojis for her, everything was always perfectly spelt, too.

'But of course Thomas didn't steal it!' Joe texted back, feeling sick. *'I hope you told Barty that.'*

'Well yes I did, but I don't know, Joe. At first I was sure he hadn't taken it, but the more I think about it, the more I don't know. Thomas's gone and locked himself in the

pod. He won't talk to anyone, just like when he was little.'

'Well I think I'd like to lock myself away from everyone if I'd been falsely accused!' Joe replied.

'But what if Thomas *did* do it, Joe? And he's locked the pod because he doesn't want anyone to search it and find the watch? We all know he's hard up, and do you remember how naughty he was when he was little, and he brought home all the animals from his friend's toy farm, hidden in his pockets?'

'Yes,' Joe replied despairingly, '*but that was just because he loved animals so much!'*

'Oh Joe,' Maggie replied, and he could just imagine the heavy sigh she was breathing as she did so. '*What do you think we should do?'*

Joe was relieved that, as they were communicating through text, he didn't have to reply immediately. It gave him a bit of time to think. Hastily he gathered his things together, crept out of the shed, and hurried off down the street.

*

Thomas had been disappointed and rather concerned to find there was still no sign of his father when he got back to the pod. Amidst all the turmoil of the missing watch, and the subsequent accusations of theft, he was worried about his dad. Especially as, on closer inspection, his sleeping-bag seemed to have gone, too. OK, so the Rover was still there, which should have been a relief, but somehow wasn't all that reassuring. Dad seemed to have been in a strange mood lately. And Thomas felt his father's absence keenly. If Dad was here, he might have reassured him, Thomas, and told him everything would be OK. Better still, he might've gone round to see that tosser, Barty and give him an expletive-laden piece of his mind. Though that didn't really sound like his father, somehow.

The thought did briefly cross Thomas's mind as to whether his father's disappearance was connected with the disappearance of the watch. But, no, he thought. Surely his dad wouldn't do that to him.

Despite the warmth of the day, Thomas turned the key in the door, locking himself into his pod. Only then did he feel safe, as if no-one could get at him. For ventilation, he opened the window at the back of the pod as wide as it would go. A small amount of breeze came in. It seemed criminal to be locking himself away on a beautiful day like this. Hopefully he could sneak out for a walk in the woods later on, and see if he could spot those elusive chiff chaffs.

Thomas lay down on his lilo and cuddled his oversized toy seal. He felt hurt and angry that he'd been accused of doing something that he simply hadn't done. A strong sense of injustice burned within him, and just like when he was a boy, his solution was simply to cut himself off from everyone and everything till he felt better enough to cope with it all. Everyone could go to hell for all he cared.

*

Joe trudged along, feeling like absolute scum. His son was being blamed for something he hadn't done, and it was all his fault. And yet he was terrified of returning to face the music. Joe had only walked a few hundred yards from the 'Woman Cave' when an idea came to him. It was quite a risky strategy, but then, he reasoned, desperate times required desperate measures. Leaning against a wall, Joe took out his phone and typed a text to Barty: *'Barty, I know it wasn't Thomas who stole your watch. In fact, I'm pretty certain that I know who did steal it. All the best, Joe'* Having pressed send on this cryptic message, he felt marginally better. Now, having cleared his head slightly, he decided it was high time he 'pulled himself together'.

Joe made his way purposefully into town, rucksack on back. When he got there, he found the town was bustling; it seemed to be market day. As he approached the plaza in the centre he could hear a stall-holder shouting repeatedly, "Strawberry, raspberry, blueberry, 2 for £3! Get your strawberry, raspberry, blueberry, 2 for £3!" Joe's strained nerves made him uncharacteristically tetchy – he felt like telling the man to shut the hell up, which he knew wasn't fair. Instead he went up to the man and bought some strawberries and blueberries, thinking the vitamin C might stop him from getting scurvy, or something, seeing as his diet could become quite limited over the next few days.

Next Joe made his way to *Mountain Warehouse,* where he purchased the cheapest one-man tent he could, for £29.99. It was called a 'Festival Tent', and was coloured bright blue and green. Slinging this purchase over his shoulder, in addition to the rucksack, Joe then ventured into *Poundland,* another first for him - Maggie didn't really approve of such places. The place was buzzing – or 'popping off', as Thomas would say, Joe thought with a pang. He was amazed at the variety of things for sale. There was even a clothing section called *'Pep & Co',* which although it wasn't £1, was still pretty cheap. Joe bought himself three new T shirts and a pack of underwear. Now he would be able to ring the changes with his new jeans, boots and jacket.

Now to the next priority - he was hungry, craving something sweet. There was a bakery next to *Poundland,* called Dee Dee's. However when Joe went inside there was a sign on the counter saying, 'SORRY, NO CAKES TODAY.' What, no cakes in a bakery? Joe frowned, wondering more than ever whether the world had gone a bit mad. His heart briefly leapt when he saw a solitary scone sitting on a plate in the glass cabinet, but the woman behind the counter shook her head apologetically. "I'm afraid I can't sell it to you, love," she said. "It's six weeks old. It's for display purposes only." Joe thought he might be prepared to have a go at a six week old scone, but the woman seemed reluctant and he didn't want to push the issue. Sighing, Joe popped back into *Poundland,* where he purchased a Tuna and Sweetcorn sandwich instead.

His purchases completed, it was time to move onto the next task on his agenda, pitching the tent. On the way into town Joe had spotted an ideal location for it. Sadly, he knew there were only too many people living rough in this economic climate. (What a mess the world – and more specifically, this country - was in.) But he'd found a place that would do for himself that didn't seem to be taken yet. It was a narrow strip of grassy land with a scattering of trees, behind a wire fence between a pavement and a parking lot - *Hilliers Street Car Park, Pay and Display.* Slowly and painfully, Joe put up his tent, following the instruction leaflet to the letter. He hadn't had to do anything like this since being roped into a camping trip with the Year 8s a couple of years ago, and even then the kids had been much better at it than him. He made an attempt to conceal his tent behind a couple of scrubby trees. Well, he thought as he sat despondently inside his blue and green polyester dome, and listened to a car zoom past a little too close for comfort. This was certainly a poor man's version of the wilds of Wales. He couldn't even get that right. What a failure he was.

*

Lucy had texted Thomas to check if he was OK. '*I know you didn't take the bloody watch, lil bro,*' she said. '*Barty can be a right shit sometimes. Do you want me to come over and hang out with you for a bit?*'

'*No thanks, Sis, I'm fine, but it's good to know you*

have my back,' Thomas texted back. *'I'm about to sneak out for a walk in the woods, but don't tell anyone, OK? Mum's already been sniffing around the pod, trying to peer through the curtains.'*

It was a funny old day, what with all this 'watch' business, and Lucy feeling sick with guilt whenever she gazed at Barty and thought of what she and Seb had done last night. She was actually relieved that there was no-one much around at the moment - Barty was sulking in the bedroom, and Maggie and Bel had gone to the playground with Fox. Dad was still AWOL of course, while Seb had last been seen disappearing into the bathroom, from where the shower could be heard running furiously and steam could be seen escaping beneath the door. Lucy found Florence relaxing on one of the chairs on the sunlit balcony, drinking a glass of orange juice. She was wearing a pale green sundress, tied in a bow under the chest. Her short, dark blonde hair was slicked back as it often was and she had little or no make-up on. The paleness of the green complemented Florence's tanned skin perfectly and Lucy thought again how pretty she was. Lucy felt quite overdressed in her long, lilac tulle skirt and white blouse, and her hair hanging loose around her neck made her feel hot.

"Hi Lucy," Florence greeted her. "Come join me, it's nice out here. Away from all the hurly-burly and insanity."

Lucy's stomach jolted, and she felt a little awkward at the prospect of being alone with Florence.

Despite Seb's assurances that he and Florence were just friends, Lucy was still not at all sure as to what exactly their relationship was. Barty had referred to her as 'Seb's ladyfriend', and they *did* share a room. She had to fight an impulse to flee from the balcony, back into the safety of the lodge.

"Hi, Florence," she smiled instead, forcing herself to sit down on the nearest free chair. She tried to relax, turning her face to the sun. Florence was right – it did feel like another world out here, peaceful, at one with nature. You could almost forget all the stress about the missing watch, Barty accusing Thomas, and Lucy's own infidelity.

Florence smiled, putting down her empty glass. "Well, it's another beautiful day, isn't it?" She gazed towards the lake, the sprinkling fountain, and the abundance of waterfowl. "We've been so lucky."

Lucy nodded her agreement. "We really have," she concurred. Then she realised she had been handed an ideal opportunity to find out something she really needed to know. She cleared her throat. "Florence –" she blushed, uncertain of how to continue. "This is kind of a delicate question, but could I just ask you something –"

"Yup, go ahead."

"What exactly is your relationship with Seb?"

Florence's face – which had been looking slightly concerned – relaxed into a look of wry amusement. "Oh, my relationship with Seb? Well it's kind of a fluid thing."

What did she mean by that, Lucy wondered? "You've known eachother a while?" she probed gently.

Florence nodded. "Oh, ages. His mother was friends with mine. We've just always hung out. We always had similar interests, you see – nature, the outdoors, environmental activism of course. It worked out quite well," she went on, "seeing as I was never a particularly girly girl."

It did make sense when she put it like that. Lucy cleared her throat delicately. She still didn't feel she had found out very much about their relationship. "So are you – just friends?"

Florence laughed at Lucy's awkwardness. "We're close, we look out for eachother when we're on protests. OK, so we're friends with benefits – very occasional benefits, these days, I have to say," she chuckled. "We have an agreement that we can see other people, whoever we want to, so I can see any men – or women – as I choose." She paused. "So that's what I mean when I say it's fluid."

"Oh, I see." Lucy was intrigued. "Sounds cool, as long as you're both OK with it."

Florence nodded. "We are." She went on, in a more confidential tone, "Don't worry, Luce. I know why you were asking about mine and Seb's relationship." She lowered her voice discreetly. "You and him are having a 'thing' together."

Lucy's heart leapt into her mouth. "Oh God, Florence. Well, of course you know." She blushed. "He's bound to have told you – you're best friends. You must hate me, for sticking my oar in like that."

Florence shook her head. "Don't be silly, of course I don't hate you. And I told you that Seb and I are chill. Plus it's hard to feel sorry for Barty, when he's so – entitled. And when he's been treating poor Thomas like shit – sorry. That's your partner I'm talking about."

"Don't worry about it," Lucy murmured. "I know exactly what you mean."

Florence paused. "Anyway, Seb really likes you, I can tell."

Lucy's face flooded with heat. She was delighted by the other woman's words, but of course she felt horrible at the same time. "Shit, Florence," she blurted. "I knew it was so wrong, getting involved with him like that. But I just couldn't help myself."

Florence's mouth twisted. "Well, yeah, life can be like that sometimes. I guess you just have to go with the flow."

"But I don't usually do stuff like that! I know that sounds like bullshit, but it's true." While her thoughts churned, Lucy gazed absently at a couple who were fishing across the lake. As the sun beat down on her head, Lucy felt as if she may be going a little crazy. "Perhaps there's something in the water round here," she suggested. "All sorts of weird stuff seems to be happening lately. Everyone's behaving out of character." Florence nodded sympathetically. She was very easy to talk to; Lucy really liked her. She felt that, in different circumstances, they could have been good friends.

"You know, I can see why Seb likes you so much," Florence continued. She stared into Lucy's eyes, and at that moment Lucy felt that she could see into her very soul. "Apart from the fact that you're nice – you're really pretty." And then Florence leaned forward, her face serious, and kissed Lucy gently on the lips.

Lucy's lips tingled, and she felt taken aback, but happy. She noticed that Florence's lips were now the colour of her own lipstick. "You're really pretty too," she said, then realised how inane it sounded.

Florence glossed over the compliment. "Thanks. I hate to cut off a beautiful friendship in its prime, but actually, that was a goodbye kiss."

Lucy felt startled, and bereft. "Why? Are you leaving?"

"Mm-hmm. I'm going to head off later today."

"Oh gosh. It – it's not because of me and Seb, is it?"

Florence shook her head. "No, silly. I want to rest up at home for a bit, enjoy all the comforts. And I miss my mum."

"Fair enough, I suppose. But *I'll* miss you," Lucy said, childishly.

Florence gave her a wry smile. "Give me your

number. We can message, and maybe even meet up at some point in the future, if the mood takes us."

Eagerly, Lucy gave out her number, and keyed Florence's into her own phone.

"Be careful, Lucy," Florence said finally. "I don't want Seb to fuck up your life – or break your heart."

Despite the warmth of the day, Lucy gave a little shiver of foreboding. "When you say 'fuck up my life', what d'you mean exactly?"

Florence shrugged. "Well I don't know – get you pregnant or something."

Lucy gave an ironic smile. "Well at least that's one thing I *don't* have to worry about."

Florence frowned. "How so? Oh, no, sorry," she added hastily. "You don't have to answer that. It's just me being nosy."

"Oh, it's fine," Lucy said. For the first time in many years, she realised that she felt like confiding. Something she had never confided to anyone else, other than the shrink. The kiss the two of them had shared seemed to have brought them closer. And Florence was leaving soon so it scarcely mattered anyway...

"Well, the thing is," she began, "I was a bit wild in my younger years..."

CHAPTER 8

Lucy had been a good, well-behaved girl, until suddenly, at the age of sixteen, she rebelled. Up till that point she had grumbled a bit from time to time, but on the whole she'd lived her life in placid acceptance, doing exactly what her parents expected of her. Which was mainly studying and doing wholesome family stuff together.

"You're so clever, Lucy," her mum would say, sycophantically. "Keep up this studying, and you'll be able to apply to Oxbridge one day!" At first, this was incentive enough. But at some time during her seventeenth year, Lucy suddenly felt she couldn't take any more of this endless *hothousing*. Her life was dull, completely controlled by her parents, and, suddenly, she yearned for freedom. Suddenly she saw how limited her parents were – they were too middle class, too unambitious, too boring. They seemed totally happy to be stuck in the comfortable rut of their jobs as teachers, content with their lukewarm, passionless marriage.

Maggie and Joe were crazy – nauseatingly so - about teaching. It was part of the whole ethos of their characters, in fact Lucy felt it was their main character trait. Not only did they spend all day doing it, but they focused a great deal of their home life on it, too – in the form of nurturing their children to fully optimise their academic potential. In practical terms for Lucy and Thomas, this had meant rigidly organised homework schedules, no socialising with friends until work was completed, and – the biggie - they didn't have a TV. Lucy was particularly gutted about this. Thomas didn't mind so much, as he was too obsessed with animals and nature to miss sitting on the sofa staring at a screen. Probably the only thing he would've wanted to watch anyway was *Springwatch,* or some shit like that. But Lucy would have loved to watch *Game of Thrones, Gossip Girl,* or *TOWIE,* to name but a few. Neither was she allowed any fripperies and trashy goods like her friends had – fluffy pink handbags, high heels, mini skirts, cheap make-up. And they had never as a family been to McDonald's – her mum banned all junk food, believing that a healthy body made for a healthy mind.

At first, Lucy's rebellion took a subtle form. Her strategy was to continue to pretend she was playing along with it all, whilst being secretly subversive. Publicly she continued to be this wholesome, academic altruistic girl but a new, more feisty side was emerging, made devious by necessity.

"Mum," she would say, "is it OK if I go to the library with Natalie and Ellie after school?"

"Sure, love," her mum would reply with a smile, "Fine. As long as you're back by seven for dinner." Meanwhile, instead of going to the library to do schoolwork, Lucy would sneak off to McDonald's with her friends, for a forbidden cheeseburger and strawberry milkshake. And to flirt with the older boys in the year above. The combination of forbidden cheeseburgers and forbidden romance meant she had little to no appetite for her wholesome jacket potato and salad when she finally arrived home.

Slowly, by stealth, Lucy began to change her appearance. Subtly she altered her fuddy duddy clothes, folding over skirt waistbands, undoing an extra button or two. She discovered make-up - and practised applying it till she became quite expert, covering her troublesome spots, sculpting her brows, defining her cheekbones and making her lips look fuller and more pouty. Whereas she'd always thought she was ugly before, she now began to realise she could be quite pretty.

If Lucy hadn't done stuff like that, she thought she would probably have gone insane. The fact that her mum worked at the same school Lucy attended meant she could keep even more of an eagle eye on her, which really got to her at times. At least Mum just noticed the academic stuff, and seemed oblivious to the way Lucy's appearance was changing.

And once they headed into GCSE year, things really stepped up a gear. Lucy wasn't allowed out with her friends at all, at evenings or weekends, which really pissed her off, and made her sad, too. She *was* allowed a phone, though, thank God. Her well-off grandfather had bought her one for her birthday. She had her own computer, too, though it was supposed to be used for doing her homework on. Up in her room, she experimented with taking selfies in her full make-up, learning to use filters and photoshop – the pictures just showed her face, which was just as well – there were only so many different ways you could style your fuddy duddy clothes; she really needed to get some new, nicer ones. Lucy got into social media big-time, mainly Facebook, where she and her friends posted photos of themselves, and 'Liked' eachother's, in a kind of mutual admiration society. When exam time rolled around, Lucy got perfectly decent, average grades for her GCSEs, but her parents seemed dissatisfied. "I'm not saying you didn't do well, but you could've done so much better, my darling," her mum said, unable to hide her disappointment. However, perhaps inevitably, in such an academic household, she was still expected to go on and do A levels.

It was around this age, as she turned seventeen, that Lucy started to get more and more pissed off, and feel more restricted by her situation. She felt trapped, and unnoticed. She had never got much attention at school – that seemed to be reserved either for the super-intelligent ones, or the really naughty ones who were rewarded if they ever behaved themselves for a short period of time. If you were good and well-behaved *all* the time, kept your head down, you got nothing. And so she started shoplifting. Make-up, stylish, cute clothes, pretty bedding, anything she fancied. She was pretty good at it, only got caught a couple of times and managed to talk her way out of it on both occasions. Thank God her parents were never informed, they would have gone ballistic. They didn't seem to notice the new items appearing in her bedroom, either. Meanwhile, Lucy's friends were shocked, and worried. She tried to get them to join her on her stealing sprees, but they didn't want to.

Lucy felt frustrated in other ways, too. There was no chance to meet boys – other than her brother's dorky friends, who were two years younger than her, and only into animals or computers. So instead, Lucy started chatting to boys on Facebook. And then, as she turned eighteen, she found a website where you could put yourself forward as a 'sugar baby' for a 'sugar daddy', and hopefully get your foot in the door to a world of money, excitement and glamour. Lucy's heart-rate sped up at the prospect.

At first, it seemed great. The agency arranged for her to attend luxurious meals out and drinks in London with businessmen and foreign dignitaries who'd flown in. All she had to do was look pretty, smile, let them kiss you. Maybe put their arms round you, get you to sit on their lap. But Lucy would never let it go further than that. She didn't feel ready yet, and when she did go all the way, she wanted it to be with someone she loved. For now she was just happy with the extra money, the glamorous experiences and freedom, the expensive gifts the men bought her.

One of the men she met through the website –

Alex, a man in his late twenties – seemed nice. He was nothing special in the looks department, slightly overweight, and balding, but as well as being rich he was kind and attentive to her, and other than kissing, didn't seem to expect anything from her. Perhaps this was because he was already married, though many of them seemed to be. By now Lucy had dropped out of her A level courses. Told her parents she'd got a job, a flat, up in London. In fact, Alex paid for the flat for her – she didn't know why he was so good to her. It was a whole different life away from her Hampshire, suburban, puritanical family. Did her parents realise what she was up to? Was it too much for them – particularly her mother - to contemplate, did she deliberately turn her head as she didn't want to know? These were questions that would bother Lucy in the years to come.

Then Lucy began to fall for Alex. They began a sexual relationship, then Lucy became pregnant. She was terrified her parents would find out. Alex pushed for her to have an abortion; he was terrified his wife would find out. Then tragedy struck. After suffering severe stomach pains Lucy was taken to hospital. It was an ectopic pregnancy, and it had almost certainly left her infertile. Alex finished his relationship with her soon afterwards. Lucy tried to keep working with the agency, but was finding it increasingly hard. She often felt depressed which made it harder to be bright and breezy on the nights out.

On one particular occasion she met Barty, out with

a group of men in the field of politics and journalism. He was posh, and privileged, but seemed more decent than the others. They began a proper relationship, independent of the agency. Then he offered her a job on his magazine, and, as they say, the rest was history. Lucy's life, that might have gone so badly wrong, had got back on track. She and Barty fell in love, he talked of having kids one day – she didn't tell him she was infertile. She was worried he would break up with her if she did. She knew he wanted a whole brood of children, to appease his masculine ego, and look good in the photos as he tried to build his political career.

Florence had been listening raptly to Lucy's story. When Lucy had finished speaking, Florence leaned across, squeezed her hand and said, "Poor darling, you've been through so much." She paused delicately. "You realise that was 'grooming', what you went through?"

Lucy shivered slightly at the ugly word. "Yes," she said quietly. "I realise that now."

Florence looked at her intently. "Have you ever had counselling or anything about it?"

Lucy nodded. "Barty paid for me to have some privately, soon after we got together. I was a bit of a mess at that point, to be perfectly honest."

"Ah well, then I suppose the man's not so bad after all." Florence paused. "Jeez. Poor old Lucy. And I can't believe your parents were that shitty to you – they seem like such nice people on the surface! How're things between you now?"

Lucy shrugged. "Not too bad. We're not as close as we might be - and they don't know anything of what I've just told you, so please don't say anything! But we're trying to work on our relationships." If her mother had been the driving force behind the strict academic discipline of her childhood, Lucy knew her father was just as culpable, for being weak, and simply echoing what her mother said. Lucy still resented them both for it. "That was one of the reasons why we came on this holiday," she told Florence. "It was meant to be a bonding experience."

But, Lucy mused, thinking of Seb, it hadn't quite worked out like that as, throughout the holiday it seemed as though the wrong people had been bonding...

Suddenly, Seb himself appeared through the French doors onto the balcony, wet-haired and fresh from his shower. "What?" he asked, gazing at the solemn, almost accusatory faces of the two women. "I'm not interrupting anything, am I?"

There was a brief pause, then Florence said brightly, "No, nothing whatsoever!" She got purposefully to her feet. "Come along," she said to Seb. "I need you to help me pack." And she led him briskly away.

Lucy enjoyed a few minutes of blissful solitude on the balcony, which gave her a chance to relax, the sun on her face, and try and gather her scattered thoughts together. All too soon, however, there was another flurry of activity from within the lodge. It was Maggie, Bel and Fox arriving back from the playground. Maggie came out to the balcony and plumped down next to Lucy, taking the seat that Florence had recently vacated. Lucy instinctively stiffened.

She thought she'd better make an effort to be friendly. "Did you guys have a nice time at the park?" She found it hard to relax with her mother, especially as she'd just been dredging up all those past grievances with Florence.

"Oh yes, Fox had a great time," Maggie smiled. "Even made a couple of little friends. It's amazing how easy that is when you're young." She leaned forward, rubbing her back. "Ooh. I think I may be getting too old for this lark, though. Pushing that swing has given me backache!"

"Oh dear, poor you," Lucy commiserated. *Lucky you're unlikely to be getting a grandchild of your own any time soon,* she added mentally. She didn't mean it harshly, it was just a statement of facts.

"All that terrible palaver about the watch," Maggie went on, running a hand through her curls. "Poor Thomas being accused - goodness me I feel quite exhausted. And God alone knows where your father has got to! But hopefully he'll be back soon," she finished, clearly attempting to put a brave face on things.

"Yes, it's all a bit of a mystery," Lucy murmured

noncommittally. She had come out here onto the balcony hoping to get away from all the stresses and strains, but they seemed to be following her around.

Then Maggie cleared her throat, lowering her voice. She leaned forward to place a tentative hand on Lucy's forearm, and Lucy tried not to shrink back from the contact. "Lucy darling, I, er, I wanted to take the opportunity of this holiday to, um, clear the air between the two of us, of any bitterness over past events ..." Maggie foundered, withdrew her hand, then her face reddened, and she looked uncharacteristically discomfited. Lucy gazed mutely on, raising a questioning eyebrow, not wanting to give her mother any help. "I guess what I'm trying to say, Lucy, is that I'm sorry about not being a better mother to you, growing up. I - I realise now that I was too strict on you - well, you *and* Thomas - but you especially. I can't blame you for wanting to get out, darling, though I wish you hadn't been so young -" For a moment Maggie's eyes glistened with tears and she made a clear effort to fight them back. "Your father and I were softer on Thomas after you'd gone - he had a lot more freedoms - mainly because we didn't want to lose him as well." She gulped. "Oh, darling! I - I should have let you have more pretty things! I - I just hope it's not too late to patch things up between us!"

At last Lucy relented - it was the pitiful mention of the 'pretty things' that did it - and gave her mother a warm smile. "I really appreciate you saying that, Mum," she said seriously. Then she went over to give her mother a hug, which left Maggie pink-faced with pleasure.

"Oh dear, between me and your Aunty Bel, we've both had our failings as parents. But then," she mused, "I suppose our *own* parents were a bit dysfunctional. It was their generation, you see. Stiff upper lip, suppressing all emotion. Young people these days are much more sensible about their emotions. Oh, Lucy, you've done so well for yourself in the end. I'm so proud of you, my darling."

*

Joe sat alone in his tent. His stomach rumbled. The tuna sandwich he'd bought in town had been a long time ago. He'd eaten a few of his strawberries and blueberries but they'd given him a tummy ache. Maybe in a bit he would venture out to McDonalds again. Although perhaps he deserved to just sit here in this tent and let himself starve to death, as if he was stranded in the Alaskan wilderness, rather than a strip of land next to a parking lot.

And of course, really, he knew he should go back to the lakeside lodge and face the music.

A reply had come from Barty to Joe's cryptic message : *'Well don't keep me on tenterhooks for God's sake, Joe!! The sooner I find out who took my watch, the more chance I have of getting it back!'*

This made Joe feel uncomfortable – he didn't know what to say to Barty next - couldn't bring himself to confess just yet, so he didn't reply. There was a beep as another Barty text came – *'Joe – where have you got to old chap? Don't know if you saw my earlier message, but please, if you know ANYthing about the theft, pls get in touch, pronto!!'*

Joe slipped his phone into his rucksack so he couldn't see it any more. He was simply too cowardly to do the right thing, and acquit his son. God knew what Thomas must be going through right now. And yet Joe clung to the thought of the watch, as a symbol of his future with Rachael. He felt as if his life was slipping into chaos - he was a mockery of his former self sitting there alone in the tent in his stylish new outfit, bought during that joyful outing to Crow's Heath. What a joke. Sitting on the thin groundsheet, the hard, sunbaked soil digging into his behind, he reflected that he hadn't even contacted Rachael yet. He thought about her adorable, sweet face, framed by that amazing blue, green and yellow hair, and of how they had made love. His love for Rachael burned in his chest like indigestion. And now he had the means to secure their happiness. He unzipped the rucksack's inner pocket, took out the watch and gazed at its beautiful, unseeing, golden face. The watch that was oblivious to all the furore around its current whereabouts.

There was a ping. Oh God, not Barty again. Reluctantly, Joe got out his phone, then his heart leapt when he saw it was a text from Rachael. *'How's the holiday going, sweet man? I miss you. Do you think it'll be possible for us to meet up again?'*

Oh how Joe longed to see her! He had one more look at the watch and then put it back in the rucksack. He had stolen from Barty so he could be with the woman he loved, but he now realised it had been a huge mistake. For heck's sake, what madness had possessed him? He could see the headlines now – **Headmaster In Watch Theft Shame!** And yet the thought of being fired from his job wasn't such a horrific prospect as it should have been.

Hours passed by, overhead the sun moved across the sky, as Joe sat alone in his tent, his head in his hands. Punished by his wretchedness, enduring a kind of physical scourge, penance for his sins. He knew he'd let everyone down - Thomas of course. And Maggie - he knew he should come clean about the whole situation to his wife, as soon as possible. He should make it as clean a break, as painless as he could. His happiness with Rachael shouldn't cause someone else's unhappiness.

Then Joe thought, Oh God. Rachael! She may be mild-mannered, but she was going to be absolutely livid when she found out – both about the watch and that he'd lied to her about the divorce. She'd probably never want to speak to him again. And yet he knew he must face up to things and contact her. With trembling hands he got out his phone and retrieved Rachael's number. He messaged her, confessing everything, and telling her where he was currently holed up in his tent. The thing was, he felt as if it was only through Rachael that he could begin to find his way home.

*

Rachael received Joe's message at work, in the board game café. She'd just taken a couple their order of fish finger sandwiches and set them up with a game of *Ticket to Ride* when she heard the bleep of her phone, and felt excited anticipation that it might be Joe replying to her message. Glancing at her phone behind the counter, she saw that it was indeed a very lengthy text from Joe, but then, as she read his double confession, the bottom dropped out of her stomach. Her mouth twisted into a grimace. Groping her way towards a chair she continued to read. It was horrendous. The facts of the matter were, he was still very much married to his wife, with no agreement to divorce yet. And to make matters worse, he had stolen a valuable watch to try and fund his future life with Rachael.

Someone came to the counter to order more coffee, and Rachael got up, pinning a friendly smile to her face, trying to function as normal. However, she was in turmoil over Joe's revelations, and her thoughts were churning. Typical! She seethed. She'd been let down by men on a couple of occasions before, but she'd kidded herself that Joe was somehow different. More fool her, for being taken in by those kind eyes and that diffident manner! She never learned. Her first instinct was to drop him like a ton of red hot coals, to seal herself off from him and prevent further hurt. However the soothing repetitive action of preparing the lattes calmed her thoughts and gave her a breathing space. As she took the coffees over to the customers, she made a decision. She would go to him and hear his side of the story first, and decide how to proceed from there.

Rachael had to wait till the café closed at 6 before going to him, and that interval of time felt like purgatory. As did the short drive to the place he'd directed her to, a patch of wasteland next to Hilliers Street car park. As Rachael drove the 2CV through the summer's evening, the thoughts swirled round in her head. Generally she put a brave face on things, but Rachael was a worrier. A little voice in her head had told her this new relationship must be too good to be true, but she hadn't listened. Well, she had only herself to blame – she had known (more or less) what she'd been getting into. A solitary tear trickled down her face. The all-too-familiar anxiety descended on her, along with the gloom. The demons revisited her, telling her what a terrible person she must be, that she would sleep with a man just because she fancied him, while knowing he had a wife. Even though she had believed the couple were on the brink of a divorce, that was no excuse. Joe had behaved very badly, but Rachael could not pretend that she herself was blameless.

"Joe?" she shouted, approaching the poorly-hidden blue and green tent on the grass verge. "Joe, you idiot, what the hell have you done?" she asked, as he unzipped his tent to let her inside. Her voice was shaking, the anger and upset clearly audible.

Joe himself looked a picture of misery. A wretched figure, he sat there on the floor of his tent, his meagre belongings scattered around him. "Thanks so much for coming Rachael," he said pathetically. "I know it's more than I deserve."

In spite of herself, her sympathy was roused. She had never seen a more pitiful specimen in her life. "Look at you, you're a mess, for God's sake." She raised an arm to his face and wiped his tears rather roughly with the cuff of her rainbow sweatshirt. "Mind you, you're not the only one who's been crying," she added briskly.

"Oh God, what have I done to you?" he asked her shamefacedly. "I'm so sorry you had to discover those things by text. And all because I was too cowardly to say it to you in person."

"Hmm, yes, it was rather shitty of you." Rachael glanced downwards, trying to gain control of her emotions. Finally she raised her eyes to his again. "Joe," she said. "I won't lie, I feel devastated and absolutely fuming with you right now. I can't believe you lied to me about your wife agreeing to a divorce!"

Joe took in a deep gulp of air. "I know, I've messed up big time. I did try to talk to Maggie about a divorce but she wasn't ready to hear it. But I thought if I told *you* that, I might lose you. But now I'm probably going to lose you anyway."

Rachael took a deep breath. "So, let's get this clear,

Joe - are you going to stay with your wife?"

"No," Joe answered, suddenly finding his backbone. "No, I am not. I know that it's absolutely over, from my point of view at least. Maggie wanted to wait until after the holiday to discuss the divorce, but I'm starting to see it's of the utmost urgency."

"*OK.*" Rachael seemed to take a deep, steadying breath. "So there was *that,*" she said. "And then you stole this chap – your friend's – watch?" He nodded. "Joe," she said, "you absolute, bloody - idiot!" She repeated the insult she had used earlier, as it seemed the only appropriate word to describe him right now.

"Yes – I know it sounds like madness – but, you see, Rachael - darling Rachael - this was my thinking - I felt *we* needed the money so much more! You and me. To build our dream life. I suppose I wasn't quite in my right mind," he went on miserably. "The thing is, Barty's so rich, he's got a whole collection of expensive watches for God's sake, that I didn't even think he'd notice if one went missing. But he *did* notice. And - and he accused my son of having stolen it."

"Oh my God," Rachael gasped. "Your poor son!" She sat up suddenly straight and resolute, surely a couple of inches taller than usual. "Now listen to me, Joe, you need to get yourself back there right now and sort things out!"

"But I can't," Joe moaned despairingly. "I'm too much of a coward. I know I'm meant to be a respectable, level-headed headmaster, a pillar of the community and all that but that's just bullshit. Like I said when I first met you, I'm a mess."

Rachael gazed up at Joe's handsome, tear-stained face. Pity stirred within her once again. She reached up and stroked back his silver-streaked hair. "Joe, you shouldn't hate yourself. You have many good qualities. Deep down, you're not a bad person, you've just taken a couple of wrong turns. You're a kind person, and an interesting person - I could talk to you for hours. And you know," she added softly, "I hate myself too, sometimes - I mean, look at me. I knew that you still had a wife. But I still slept with you. I fancied you, so I chose to ignore my conscience."

Joe shook his head vehemently. "No. Rachael, you're so good. That's why I love you. You trusted me and believed me. The fault for what's happened is completely mine."

Rachael felt a little boosted by the evident depth of Joe's feelings. But it alarmed her the way he was quite so down on himself, even though he had behaved very badly. "You know, *I* get depressed too," she went on, in her quiet, calm voice. "And it's because counselling helped pull me out of it – that, along with medication - that I decided to train as a counsellor myself – to pay it forward, as they say."

Joe gazed at her in loving concern. "You get depressed too? Oh, my poor darling."

"So, yes, like I say I have my coping strategy, there's the medication, the counselling, and then just keeping it all going on a day-to-day basis. I'm no expert, but from my own experience you must eke the little pleasures out of life. A last cup of tea before bed, whilst looking at your phone. Laying in bed for an extra 15 minutes in the morning, eating toast and butter. Snuggling up in bed at night with a good book. A chocolate biscuit with a cup of coffee. It's all about looking after yourself."

"It sounds good. Maybe -" He paused. "Maybe we could look after eachother?" Then he added in a rush, "No, that's not going to be happening after what I've done."

Rachael sighed. "You *can* make up for what you've done, Joe," she said, "if you will just go back."

Joe took a deep breath. "I know. I know I must." He closed his eyes, and swayed slightly.

"Joe?" Rachael frowned, laying a hand on his shoulder. "Are you OK?"

"A little peckish," he murmured. "I was meaning to pop out to McDonalds for dinner but then..."

Rachael tutted, with considerable exasperation. "For heck's sake, you really are hopeless." She fetched her bag, and got out a tub containing the leftovers from the café – a couple of slices of tomato and broccoli quiche, and some mint choc chip cake, complete with fluorescent green icing. "I'm not sure you deserve it," she said, shoving it towards him. "But there you go."

CHAPTER 9

It was about 8pm and Barty was in his bedroom trying to relax with a brandy, while Lucy sat nearby at the dressing table taking her jewellery off. Suddenly his phone bleeped, heralding a text from Joe. Well, it was a bit of a bombshell, actually, in which the man confessed that *he* had stolen the Patek Philippe. There was a photo of the watch attached to the message, to prove the truth of what he was saying.

"Well I'll be buggered," Barty exclaimed, sagging back in his desk chair in a combination of relief and anger. "Sorry to have to break it to you, Muffin, but it seems your blasted father was behind the theft all along – all that cloak-and-dagger stuff earlier about 'knowing who the real culprit was', combined with the fact that he'd gone AWOL – hmm, I smelled bullshit from the get-go. Still, I wouldn't have thought the man would have the gumption." Barty paused, re-reading the message. "He says he'll be back first thing tomorrow, damned cheek – pity I don't know where he's holed up, or I'd be up there like a shot, beating fifty shades of crap out of him." Barty had been a leading light in the amateur boxing club at university, and liked to fancy he was still pretty good at it.

Lucy was deeply shocked by the news of her

father's behaviour, but she did her best to retain an appearance of calm. "Goodness, I'd rather you didn't hurt him, Barty. He *is* my dad, after all. Speaking of my family," she went on, frowning, "don't you think you'd better pop round to the pod and say sorry to my brother for having falsely accused him?"

"Hmm. Well yes, I suppose so," Barty said grumpily. "If you really think that's a priority."

"Yes, I do. And while you're about it," Lucy added, "I've got an idea of the perfect way for you to make it up to Thomas."

Barty recognised this mood of Lucy's, and that steely look in her eyes. "Oh really?" he sighed. "And what might that be, Muffin?"

*

Thomas had greatly enjoyed his earlier walk in the woods. It had left him feeling calmer; much better. Seeing the minutiae and at the same time the enormity of the natural world had helped to put everything in perspective. Silly, trifling human cares. What did it matter who was in current possession of a contraption of metals and diamonds? What did the hare or the badger in the forest care about designer branding?

Thomas had enjoyed spending the entire day on his own, and was now less than delighted to hear the crunch of heavy, approaching feet on the gravel, and see the large, red-faced shape of Barty looming up through the French doors. He unlocked the pod, and listened while Barty delivered his apology and declared Thomas's exoneration in typical stuttering, rambling fashion. "Which is, you know, woo-hoo!" the shambolic, red-haired man finished, punching the air upwards in that way he had.

However, as well as being in a state of shock at his father's guilt, Thomas had been too badly hurt to accept Barty's apology graciously. "Well I'm pleased for you that you're getting your watch back," he said. "But sorry doesn't really cut it, I'm afraid. So," he concluded, "as far as I'm concerned, you can stick your apology up your arse."

At this point, left to his own devices, Barty would have turned on his heel and stormed off back to the lodge, mortally offended. However, he remembered his instructions from a stern-faced Lucy, and gritted his teeth. "I was, er, thinking there might be something I could do to make it up to you, Thomas my fellow," he said. "How would you feel about a job on the old mag, writing a weekly section covering all matters related to wildlife and climate change? And you could always use your maths skills to set some mathsy puzzles, too – logic problems, that kind of thing."

Thomas's brown eyes widened. "Really? Maths *and* wildlife? *Now* you're talking, Barty my old chum." He reached out to shake Barty's hand.

*

Meanwhile Joe was yet to make his way 'home',

having decided he should endure at least one night in the tent. As a kind of rite of passage. Rachael had offered to take him home to her boat, just to sleep, not for a night of passion, she'd clarified. An offer which, though cosy and tempting, Joe declined. He felt it was only by staying in the tent that he would prove he was 'up to it', that he really was cut out for a simpler life. He also felt that the discomfort might serve as some kind of punishment for his crimes. Full of Rachael's quiche and mint chocolate cake, Joe crept outside to take a last pee into the bushes before settling down for the night. Despite the heat of the day, it was surprisingly cold tonight. Back in the tent, he swapped his black blazer jacket for a grey zip-up fleece that he'd brought with him, added an extra pair of socks, and wriggled into his sleeping bag. With no airbed, the ground was iron-hard beneath his body, and he knew he'd probably have backache by morning. His phone had run out of charge and there was nothing to do, nothing to distract him from his solitude, from himself, his thoughts, here at large in the world. Joe felt suddenly exposed on his grass verge, where he could hear cars zooming past every few minutes. But this was a fear that homeless people had to deal with every night. Then he experienced a momentary twinge of worry that a gang of drunken yobs might break into his tent and murder him in the night. Jeez, get a grip, Joe! he told himself. He shouldn't be such a wuss, and really, he was dog-tired, and the thoughts soon drifted away, as he laid still, clearing his mind ready for sleep. He was going to need a good night's rest if he was to be fit to face everyone the following day.

*

Early the following morning, Joe packed his tent up and made his way back to the Lakeside Park via a combination of public transport and hitching rides. It was a nerve-wracking and time-consuming journey - people seemed even less eager to give him lifts than they had been on his outward journey – but then he could see why, as his clothes had become very rumpled and his hair was in dire need of a wash.

When he finally tottered in through the doorway of the lodge, everyone was far nicer to him than he deserved. No-one pounced on him or physically attacked him. No-one bombarded him with an angry tirade of words. There were just various hurt or disappointed glances in his direction. Maggie glanced at him silently and reproachfully as if to say, '*How could you have done that to our son?*' Joe gulped, vowing to have a proper chat with her later. Lucy came up to him and looked at him searchingly and said, "Oh, *Dad,* what the hell have you been playing at?" Then she enfolded him in a hug.

Emerging from Lucy's embrace, Joe took off his rucksack, unzipped the inner pocket, took out the watch and placed it into Barty's outstretched hands. The heavy watch pooled into his cupped hands, and Barty stared at the item hungrily, almost fanatically.

"I'm so sorry, Barty," Joe said quietly. "Is there

somewhere we could have a chat?"

"Certainly. Follow me," Barty said, and led him to his bedroom. Joe followed, feeling as if he was walking to the scaffold. He felt at a distinct disadvantage. He was grimy and wretched from his exploits; Barty meanwhile was clean and immaculate. Barty sat at the advantageous position of his desk chair, while Joe sat on the squishy bed, like a disgraced schoolchild. What if Barty decided to press charges, Joe fretted? Well, that was his prerogative, of course.

Thankfully the thought of Rachael made Joe feel strong enough to face the ordeal ahead. She had given him some tips on how to face Barty. He pictured her face, solemn and earnest, framed by the green and yellow hair. "First thing," she'd said, "Apologise from the heart. Second: Take responsibility, own the mistake. Be honest, explain that you think you've been suffering from stress, and you're planning to see a doctor about it. But don't make excuses for yourself. Third, Explain exactly why you did what you did, so he can follow your thought process."

So Joe went through the whole sorry story - editing out certain details such as meeting Rachael and his wish to divorce Maggie. "I've been feeling a bit depressed lately," he began, his hands trembling in his lap. Well, that was an understatement. "I wanted a way out, a change of direction. I needed some money – fast - to fund a new life. So I stole your watch." He tried to keep it vague, so that Barty would not suspect about his tumultuous love life. "I know it was very wrong."

Barty frowned. "What exactly are you getting at, fella? You 'needed some money fast'? Is it gambling? Alcoholism? Or you want to buy a VW Camper so you and Maggie can chuck in your jobs and go travelling round Europe?"

Joe squirmed, feeling himself pinned down, like the unwilling subject of one of Barty's magazine interviews. "I'm really sorry, Barty, but I can't explain exactly right now. There are people I have to talk to first, like Maggie –"

"I *see*," Barty said, raising an eyebrow.

His expression put the fear of God in Joe. Crikey, talk about letting the cat out of the bag! Barty would probably twig about the divorce, and then he would tell Lucy, who might in turn tell Maggie... Joe glanced down at his lap, seeking escape. "I don't know how I could have been so stupid," he blurted out. "Especially when you've been kind to me, Barty, and a friend."

"Hmm, yes, well, I've a good mind to press charges," Barty said, and Joe's stomach shrivelled. "But I'm not going to," Barty went on. He raised a gingery eyebrow. "You have your wife and daughter to thank for that. You know how feisty Lucy is in defending things she loves. And Maggie in particular was quite insistent that involving the police would cause you to lose your job, and therefore ruin your life."

Joe took a sharp intake of breath. How ironic, he thought, that Maggie had been so loyal, defending him to Barty, when it was the last thing he deserved.

"Thank you, Barty," Joe said.

"Besides which," Barty went on, "you cut a pretty wretched figure anyway."

Barty's assessment was not wrong. Joe's heart pounded, he felt hot and flustered. He felt terrible for his treatment of Maggie, and knew that their chat could not come soon enough. So many people to apologise to... so little time.

Barty was staring at him in mild disdain. "Now for God's sake, man, go and get yourself a shower and some clean clothes, before I have to open a window in here."

*

An hour or so after her father's eventful return, Lucy was lying on a picnic blanket on the grass outside the lodge. It was the perfect place to de-stress, the only sound the playful splash of the fountain in the lake. She was wearing a pink floral print halter dress which was quite short, the briefest thing she had brought with her, but had put plenty of sun cream on and was enjoying the feel of the sun on her skin. She was holding her phone above her and gazing up at it, checking her social media - she knew she should really be doing something 'improving', like reading the copy of James Joyce's *Ulysses* that she had brought in her suitcase. But she was feeling overwhelmed by everything that had happened within the last few hours, and felt like giving her mind a rest.

Suddenly a long, dark shadow fell over her. Feeling

vulnerable, Lucy immediately scrambled up to a sitting position, then felt relieved when she saw who it was.

"Hey," said Sebastian. "Where is everyone? I mean, I know Florence has gone home, but what about the others?"

He looked bloody gorgeous as usual, Lucy thought, dark-haired and dashing, exhibiting that eclectic sense of style once again, in a black sweatshirt and black-and-white checked trousers. He always seemed to stay cool as a cucumber, despite the hot weather.

"Oh, hi," she managed. Lucy's stomach did a little flip, but she was careful not to show any outward emotion, despite the fact that it made her feel unaccountably excited being alone with him. Barty had yet to voice any suspicions about her and his son, but she felt as if he had been watching her like a hawk ever since the night of the circus. And that in turn affected how she interacted with Seb. And another part of her wondered if she could trust him, after that veiled warning from Florence - ('*I don't want Seb to fuck up your life – or break your heart'*...) "To answer your question," she went on, "my dad and Thomas have gone for a walk and a chat." Her voice was deceptively steady. "Barty's in the bedroom, supposedly working on his book, my mum's gone to visit the Museum of Sewing Machines in Haughton – rather her than me - and I think Bel and Fox have popped over to the circus to watch Sophy perform in the matinee - Bel said something about wanting to clear the air with her afterwards."

"Wow, that seems to be everyone and their motivations thoroughly accounted for." Their eyes met and something flashed between them, a spark of connection, a sparkle of amusement. "I don't know how you manage to tabs on everyone's movements like that, very impressive," Seb said. He flung himself down on the red tartan blanket, to half-lie, half-sit beside her, close enough that their hands were touching. Lucy knew she should edge a respectable distance away from him, but she didn't want to.

He looked at her. "I like that dress. You have great shoulders. Square. Powerful. Sexy. I don't think I've seen them before."

"Thanks," she said. She'd been a bit self-conscious about her shoulders in the past. "Florence has nice shoulders, too," she heard herself saying, remembering them. "They're very dainty, and smooth."

"True," Sebastian agreed. He glanced away from her. He seemed slightly nervous, edgy. "Luce, About the other night, when we went to the circus –" Lucy knew he wasn't referring to the show they'd seen, but what they'd done afterwards.

She met his gaze. "It was good," she said, getting hot under the collar at the memory. "OK, it was amazing."

He smiled. "*You* were amazing," he said. "It was a bit unplanned. It just kind of happened. I'm glad it was OK for you." He frowned. "But you were definitely protected, right?" he went on in a low voice, looking at her. "You're definitely not pregnant?" There was an odd note of hope in his voice, Lucy thought, almost as if he wished she *was* pregnant. She decided she must be imagining it.

"No," Lucy sighed wearily, "I'm definitely not pregnant." She briefly imagined what a child made by her and Sebastian might look like. It made her feel quite emotional for a moment.

"Oh. OK. Cool." Seb started picking the daisies that grew in the grass around the blanket, and began to make a daisy chain. "I'm probably off on my next protest soon," he said casually, threading a daisy through the stem of another. "We're focusing on another part of the new rail route next, up in Staffordshire. I know you mentioned that you wanted to get involved in environmental stuff. How would you feel about coming with me?"

Lucy was shocked by the question. "What, leave Barty, you mean?"

Seb shrugged. "Depends. I mean there are a couple of ways we could play it." He pierced the stem of a daisy with his thumbnail, releasing a spurt of green juices.

Lucy's cheeks flooded with heat. "So, you're saying either leave Barty officially, make a clean break, or tell him I'm going on a protest with you, under the guise of being just friends?" She had lowered her voice, aware that Barty was only a few metres away, and could possibly hear them through his bedroom window. "Or, the third option, actually go as genuinely just friends, with everything very proper and above board."

Sebastian nodded. "Something like that. Though I don't think I could stand to be just friends with you," he frowned. "So that particular option is out."

He had such a dramatic turn of phrase, she thought. It was like living in a novel written by one of the Brontes. And it was catching - Lucy's own emotions churned with her dilemma. Passion flared whenever she so much as looked at Sebastian, but the thought of abandoning Barty for him tugged painfully at her heartstrings. She knew she had already behaved unforgivably by having an affair with Seb. Guilt haunted her 24/7 - at night the glow sticks still glimmered provocatively from her bedside table, though they were fading fast. Lucy was genuinely attached to Barty; she had real feelings for him; and their life together was very pleasant and companionable. And what about Barty himself, how would *he* feel if she were to abandon him? Leaving him for Sebastian would be a particularly shitty thing to do, as it was his son. *Would* Barty be utterly devastated if she left him, she wondered, or was she just eye candy to him, a pretty accessory to be in his photos for *Hello* magazine? Would he quickly find someone else to replace her?

"I love you," Sebastian said, his voice intruding

into her thoughts, as he repeated his declaration of the night of the circus. Lucy's heart gave a little jolt. "What could be more natural than for us to be together?" he added.

Lucy's brow furrowed in consternation. What would life with Seb be like, she wondered? Lucy sensed it would be passionate but tumultuous. She recalled Florence's warning - what did it mean? Had he broken Florence's heart at some point?

"What about Florence?" Lucy asked. "She's the one you usually go to protests with."

"She could still join us," Sebastian shrugged. "She'd be cool. She likes you."

"Well it's mutual, because I like *her*."

Seb raised his eyebrows, and Lucy raised hers back.

Having completed his handiwork, Seb reached out and placed the daisy chain crown onto Lucy's head, on top of the plaited crown that Fox had already done her. His fingers brushed against her scalp as he did so, where the sensory neurons shot a rapid message to her brain's pleasure centre. "Thanks," Lucy smiled. She used the selfie camera on her phone to check how the flower crown looked, and adjusted it slightly. "I love it!"

"Anyway, back to the subject of the protest," Sebastian said impatiently. "Will you come? Come away with me?"

Seeking relief from the churning of her thoughts,

Lucy decided to play devil's advocate. "Do you ever wonder if you're doing the right thing by protesting? I mean, what about what my mum said in the King's Head that first night?" she asked. "About the protests disrupting the lives of ordinary people? I mean, it *must* be stressful if you're trying to drive to work and someone has superglued themself to the road in front of you. And you hear about people practically coming to blows. I'm not sure if I'm brave enough to be that person glued to the road!"

"But *someone* has to be brave and put themselves on the line, if they want to bring about change!" Sebastian said. "You may not always win a popularity contest for it. And like I said before, it's the government that tricks us into thinking it's the ordinary person versus the protestor. When really we're all on the same side, against the government, and big business."

Lucy nodded, tired now of being the provocateur. "I must admit, I do agree with you. My mum's an intelligent woman. But sometimes she's too trusting of things she reads in the papers or hears on certain news channels. Maybe it's a generational thing. Perhaps having had access to the internet from a young age means you're more sceptical because you're constantly exposed to a whole spectrum of opinions."

"I think you're right," Seb said earnestly. "About maintaining a healthy scepticism. It's a mistake to blindly trust the powers that be. I mean, you already know that. You work on a political magazine for God's sake."

"Well yes, it's true that politicians portray a certain version of events, not the absolute truth. But then, doesn't everyone?" Lucy thought of all the deceit that had been happening amongst their family unit during this holiday.

"No, it's not the same thing at all!" Seb argued. Their discussion had become quite intense, their voices slightly raised as they sat there on the picnic blanket, but they were aware of nothing but eachother. "Because *they* are the ones with the power. And it's all based on money and corruption."

"Oh God, it's depressing, isn't it," Lucy sighed, "to feel the world's such a bad place? I want to believe it's full of magic and sparkle!"

Seb leaned toward her, tucking her hair behind her ear. "It would be, if we were together." Then he kissed her lingeringly on the lips.

"Seb!" Lucy reproved him gently, pulling away. "Someone could come past at any moment!"

*

Joe and Thomas were walking to the nearby village of Dragon's Green. Joe had asked his son if he would come for a walk with him, so that he could offer his apologies, and explain.

"OK," Thomas had replied, eyeing his father warily. "But don't let's talk till we get to the pub. I need a pint in my hand before I can listen to this."

And so, as they walked in silence along the narrow pavement beside the road, Joe tried to distract himself from the daunting prospect of making yet another apology. At least their surroundings were idyllic; soothing to the fevered soul. As they approached the so-called 'village', Joe thought fancifully what a simple, cute set-up they had here – just one post office slash village shop, and one pub. Right nextdoor to eachother. Whereas in Joe's home town, there was a whole multitude of chi-chi businesses of dubious usefulness. I mean, he thought, who needed five or six cafes or restaurants within a few hundred yards of eachother as they had back home – all of which seemed to follow the latest single-word naming trend - Sage, Perch, Pitch, Baked, Malt... The kind of place where, if you went to use the loo, the toilet doors were trying very hard to look like a rustic wooden shack. Maggie and Lucy loved those places of course, saying they were atmospheric, independent and served good quality food, but Joe personally thought they were pretentious and overpriced. He'd rather have a simple, no-nonsense life, like the life he'd hoped for with Rachael. Joe glanced in through the doorway of the shop as they passed, and saw a sign saying, £5 for a punnet of grapes. He winced. Hopefully the shops would be a bit cheaper in the wilds of Wales, if he ever got there.

At the King's Head, Joe went to the bar and ordered beers and lunch for him and his son. Still not talking, other than essential communications about their order, they left the low-hanging gloom of the pub to go through to the sunny garden out the back, where wooden pub benches were dotted about on the lawn, each topped with a red sun umbrella. There were only a handful of other customers. Joe took a deep breath of fresh air. You really felt as if you had escaped from everyday life here, he couldn't help thinking, the lush summer greenery of hedges and trees that surrounded the garden serving to mute the noise from the outside world, the road that ran fairly nearby.

"There's a nuthatch singing in that tree," Thomas observed. He took a long draught from his pint of beer.

"Oh, lovely." Joe sipped at his own beer. It tasted bitter, gently fizzy, and very refreshing. He put down his glass, and cleared his throat. "Look, Thomas," he began. "I'll cut to the chase. There are no excuses for what I did. The thing is, I was feeling very unhappy with the life I was living –"

"You never said!" The words were flung accusingly at him across the pub table.

"I know - and I'm really sorry, Thomas. I didn't know how to say, how to even *begin* to explain any of what I was feeling to you, or your mother, or Lucy... God, looking at it now I can see I've never really communicated effectively with you guys. I've been a pretty crap father haven't I –"

"We didn't have the easiest of childhoods, that's for sure," Thomas interjected bitterly.

"Again, you're right, of course - I can see now that your mum and I went about it all wrong. We thought we were doing the right thing - you see we were worried excessive screen time would have a negative effect on your school grades; that's why we banned the TV. And if I didn't always agree with your mum's stance - well that's my fault for not speaking up, for taking a backseat role." He sighed. "We've pretty much failed as parents. We were way too strict on the both of you. And now I've let you down again. Big time." Joe bowed his head in shame.

"And you say it's because you were fed up with your life?" Thomas asked curiously.

Joe nodded. "Like I say, I know it's no excuse."

"Indeed," Thomas said. "And besides," he added, sounding more subdued, "we all get sick of our lives sometimes."

"Yes, I'm starting to realise that," Joe said, slowly raising his head again. "And I'm sorry. I have been exceedingly selfish in all this. You're my son, and I'd want you to feel, if *you* ever needed someone to talk to, you could talk to me."

"Hmph. Maybe if you hadn't gone and betrayed me like that I might've considered it! Now I'm not sure if I'll ever trust you again." The alcohol had loosened their tongues; they were becoming more heated.

Joe tried desperately to explain his motivation. "The thing is, I stole the watch to fund a new life; a better life; I thought it would serve Barty right when he had so much and others had so little! It just never occurred to me that he would suspect *you* of stealing it, Thomas!"

Thomas's brows drew together in a frown. "Yes well I guess it was just my bad luck that I'd been showing a polite interest in the bloody thing the night before." He took another long drink of his beer. "Shit. It was bloody stupid of you, Dad. Stupid and reckless. I'd always thought of you as a sensible and *considered* kind of person before."

"I know," Joe said glumly. "I've been an idiot. I'll do anything I can to make it up to you."

"Hmm," Thomas said. "Well, I'll keep you posted on that one, I'll let you know when I decide the best way for you to make it up to me." His tone was serious, unforgiving.

The food arrived, cheese and onion toasties and a large portion of chips to share.

"So anyway," Thomas continued, helping himself to some chips. "What's this 'new life' you're on about?" He sprinkled salt, vinegar and ketchup on his chips, in that neat, methodical way he had.

Joe chewed a mouthful of toastie, washing it down with beer. How to describe the 'new life' he dreamed of – without mentioning Rachael? Because he couldn't tell Thomas about Rachael, not until Maggie knew about the situation. "It's just I -" Joe tried to explain the desperation that had been the main part of his motives. "- I'm just fed up with the way life is these days. I decided I wanted out. It got quite bad for a time back there – " he went on. "With hindsight I think I was suffering from depression." Thomas looked concerned at this, so Joe added, "I'm a bit better now, but I'm still planning to see a doctor."

"I'm glad to hear it. I haven't mentioned this before, but I'm actually on a low dose of anti-depressants myself."

"Really? Oh, God, Thomas." Joe shook his head. First Rachael, and now Thomas. He really should have known this about his own son.

"Anyway, Dad, so you were sick of your life…"

"Er. Well. Yes – not you, Thomas, it's nothing personal, I love you dearly. And Lucy."

"But Mum?"

Joe's stomach dropped slightly. "There are some issues with our relationship – but I should really be talking to her about that first – no, the main thing I was unhappy with was just Life. You know, school, college, uni, job, the way it's all like one big sausage factory. We're all crammed into the mincer, chopped up, and then squeezed out into neat little sausages at the end."

Thomas wondered if his father had gone slightly insane. Or whether the beer was going to his head. But in a way he knew where he was coming from. "Go on," he said.

"It's all a big money machine that we're tricked

into being part of," Joe surged on. "Obedience, buying." His sandwich was going cold on the plate in front of him. A couple at a nearby table looked at them a bit funny. "Everything's so expensive now. Maggie was talking about a hen do some friend of hers at work was having. It was costing thousands. I mean, when or if Lucy marries Barty, will *I* have to pay for the wedding? God knows what that would cost, the extravagant kind of do they would want. I would be tied to that wretched headmaster's job forever!"

"I'm not sure the bride's parents are still expected to cough up," Thomas said, wryly amused. "I think that idea's a bit old-fashioned now."

"Is it?" Joe asked, a tinge of hope entering his voice. "I sure hope so. It's such a waste of money, it's all so *unnecessary*. The establishment, the world system, Mass Consumerism, all conditioning us to believe that we want and need more and more stuff, so that we have to work all hours to pay for it. But we never have quite enough money, we always need more, so we're always playing catch up." Now the floodgates of his mouth had opened, there was no stopping him. It was as if after all those years of being quiet and keeping his head down, the pent-up flow was being let loose in style.

"I agree with you there," Thomas said. "I mean, as things currently stand I have little to no hope of getting my own house. I feel like I'm going to be doomed to live at home forever." Thomas usually tried to look on the bright side, but if you looked at it dispassionately, life seemed pretty bleak sometimes. He had a shit job, no place of his own, no girlfriend. He'd liked Florence, but she'd been with Sebastian, and besides, she was gone now.

"Ah yes, a fate worse than death, sharing a house with me and your mother," Joe quipped. "But no, seriously, I do feel for you. Maybe I should've kept Barty's watch," he added ruefully, "and given the proceeds to you instead."

Thomas raised an eyebrow. "Maybe," he said sarcastically. "Or perhaps I should just join you in your new life off-grid."

"Hm, yes, I wonder – maybe that could work." Joe wasn't quite sure *how* that would work out – he felt guilty that his son didn't yet know he was hoping to share his future life with Rachael, if she would have him. But maybe Thomas could be a part of the picture, too. He could have his own little place, not too far from the two of them. And Thomas would love being so close to nature. Then Joe came back to the present with a crash. "Oh God, Thomas, I've fucked up royally, haven't I?"

Thomas raised an eyebrow sardonically. "Actually there's a reason I might not be able to join you in your new off-grid life. Barty's offered me a job."

"He's *what*?"

"On his magazine, to ease his conscience. No thanks to you, Dad," Thomas added. And though his tone was jovial, his words sent little daggers into Joe's heart.

*

On his way back to the pod with Thomas, Joe was waylaid by Maggie, who'd just arrived back from the museum of sewing machines. "Ah, there you are!" she said. "About time, too. I want a word with you." Her tone was ominous.

"What, right now?" Ideally Joe would've opted for a breather at this point. He'd thought the chat with his son hadn't gone too badly. However, Maggie was another proposition altogether.

"Yes, now," she said.

"Er, OK, then." Joe knew it was the least he could do. It was high time he had a full and frank discussion with his wife.

Maggie swept Joe away, pausing to say over her shoulder, "Bye, Thomas, sweetie, see you later!"

"Oh - bye, Mum – and Dad. See ya in a bit."

"Where are we going?" Joe asked, starting to feel slightly alarmed, as Maggie marched him away.

"For a walk," Maggie replied. He fell into step with her on the footpath around the lake, but for once both of them were too distracted to admire the birds or the water. They came to a long wooden fishing jetty and Maggie wandered out onto it, Joe following obediently in her wake. If he felt a momentarily qualm about being surrounded by water, he dismissed it. His wife looked stylish in her outfit, he noticed, a black long-sleeved top and wide-legged trousers patterned with dark orange leaves. Her curls blew gently in the faintest of breezes. He'd loved her once, admired her greatly. Maggie was so capable. So clever. Beside her, he'd always felt as if he paled into insignificance. How did *he* get to be a head teacher, he mused while they walked along the jetty - while she was 'just' a head of year? Was it good, old-fashioned sexism? Sadly, Joe suspected so.

Halfway along the jetty, Maggie paused, continuing to gaze straight ahead of her. The sound of the fountain could, as always, be heard, splashing gently nearby. "Beautiful here, isn't it?" she said, gazing at the idyllic scenery, letting out a calming sigh. She strolled out further along the wooden walkway, and Joe followed her. He felt slightly anxious now, as the water was so very dark and impenetrable. He made a deliberate effort not to glance downwards.

Maggie stopped at the end of the jetty, and frowned at him. "You've been looking different since you got back from your travels," she said. "What's that outfit?"

Joe glanced down at what he was wearing. He had almost forgotten he was sporting a new look by now. And he may have changed the T shirt, but he'd been wearing the jeans and jacket for quite a few days now and was aware that it was high time he rang the changes. He'd have to visit the charity shop again, see if they had another jacket with a similar vibe; and another pair of jeans. Otherwise he'd have to sit in the campsite laundrette washing his jeans like the guy in that old Levi's advert. His mouth twisted wryly at the thought.

"What are you smiling at?" Maggie demanded. "Did I say something funny? I hardly think this is the time for levity, Joe, do you? Your behaviour has been nothing short of disgraceful. I can't believe you let our son take the blame like that."

He felt like one of her pupils being told off. He had never felt less like a headmaster himself. Right now he felt as if he had about as much authority as a flea.

The smile wiped itself off Joe's face. "No," he said, contrite. "I'm sorry, Maggie. It was a shitty thing to do. I must have been off my head. I took Thomas for lunch earlier - I've been trying to make it up to him, but I'm not sure he'll ever forgive me."

"Hmm, I wouldn't blame him." Maggie continued to observe him through narrowed eyes. "There's just something different about you," she went on. "– I can't put my finger on it. Is it the influence of another woman, causing your sartorial transformation?"

"No, it's all me," Joe said earnestly. "The clothes, that is. I chose them myself. From a charity shop."

"A *charity* shop? But you never go in charity shops."

This was it. This was his cue. "I know." He swallowed. "But I did go in there with someone I'd met. And yes, it was a woman. We – we've become friends. Well, more than friends."

There was a moment when Maggie went ominously silent. A suspicious gleam of tears glazed her eyes. Then she flung her head forward and burst out, "I *knew* it!", so loudly it scared a couple of mallard ducks away. "And yet you lied to me, swearing there was no-one else." She paused for a second to draw breath. "So you met this woman, while *we* were away on holiday, supposed to be having some quality time together –"

"I'm *so* sorry, Maggie –" This seemed to be all he was saying lately.

"Oh come on for fucks sake, give it a rest!" Maggie hissed back.

Joe steeled himself to meet her gaze. He knew that he deserved her anger; knew that so far he had got off far lighter than he deserved. "I should have talked to you properly, long ago. The fault is entirely mine – the thing is, I haven't felt as if you and I have been very happy together for a while now –"

"Speak for yourself!" She clenched her teeth grimly, narrowing her eyes. "Now it makes sense why you wanted to have a 'serious talk about divorce', after the holiday! So you could get together with this new woman of yours."

Joe knew it was time to be a hundred per cent honest with Maggie. "It's not just about Rachael –" he tried to explain.

"Rachael!" she echoed, sounding pained.

"- It's about my life in general. I'm sick of being a headmaster. I want to sell up my half of the house, and have a simpler life somewhere in the countryside –"

"Oh, do you? How nice for you." She paused ominously, before spitting out, "OK then, you can have your bloody divorce!"

Maggie took a sudden step towards him, forcing Joe to take a step backward. His heart leapt into his mouth. He was right on the edge of the jetty now, and feeling very wobbly. The beer he'd drunk at lunchtime wasn't helping. If Maggie took another step, or say she were to push him, he'd be sent straight backwards into the water. He looked desperately around him for help. The banks of the lake gazed emptily back at him. Where were all the friendly fishermen and women when you needed them? Where were the barbecue-tending neighbours? It seemed to be just him and Maggie, alone in the world, locked into this primeval, visceral struggle. Joe's heart pounded as he imagined the dark water; the mud, the tangling weeds that would pull him down...

CHAPTER 10

As she squared up to Joe, taking a grim pleasure in seeing him squirm, Maggie had a sudden moment of clarity. This was horrendous; what was she doing? She was behaving like a total psycho. She could see the fear in her husband's eyes. He'd even taken his glasses off, worried he might lose them if he fell in. Good God, she thought to herself, had she turned into some kind of monster? She knew Joe was terrified of dark water.

And then, a more profound thought struck her - was Joe even worth getting that upset about?

Standing there poised on the jetty, Maggie forced herself to take a deep, calming breath. And then forced herself to take a long, hard look at her marriage. Perhaps it was time for a reassessment. Sure, she'd assumed she and Joe would grow old together - but had that assumption made her settle for the increasing mediocrity of their relationship? Quite possibly. The thing was, what they had now was a far cry from the passion of their early days together. As she gazed at Joe, as he stood cringing there on the edge of the jetty, Maggie felt as if a weight was suddenly lifted from her shoulders. She had an epiphany, a moment of sudden blinding clarity. She might, she realised, actually be happier if they split. After all, the kids were grown now. She could move in with Bel if she wanted. It would be companionable, cosy. Maggie didn't feel too bothered about meeting another man. It occurred to her that she might be through with sex, all that hassle and complication. That she might actually *want* to be celibate. You could be anything sexually these days, couldn't you? Including asexual. It was celebrated rather than laughed at. Goodness, if her parents were still alive they would have been shocked!

The more she thought about it, the more the idea grew on her. Maggie felt as if she could certainly live without Joe's frugal and penny-pinching ways – really, he was perfectly cut out to live a sparing, basic life in the wild. She'd had enough. He'd messed her around for long enough, with his cavalier attitude towards her feelings. He had those puppy dog eyes that women went crazy for, but really, he was weak-willed and thoughtless. She felt shocked (but not upset, as it wasn't her problem) at the prospect of him chucking in his headmaster's job. But Maggie was not worried about money. She earnt good money herself anyway, she was an independent woman.

There was another plus point, too - if she no longer had Joe to consider, Maggie realised that she would be able to do all the fun things he'd never wanted to do. Go up and see a musical in town, go out and watch plays, enjoy meals at smart restaurants, trips to see the sights. There was Bel, and besides, Maggie had lots of other friends, who would be only too happy to accompany her on such pleasurable outings. As she'd said before, the children were grown, and if she had to move into a smaller place, she was happy to. She would never regret their marriage because of the kids - but neither would she mourn its ending.

Joe was still cringing on the end of the jetty. Maggie took a step back from him. "Don't look so worried. I'm not going to try and drown you." She took him briskly by the hand and dragged him back down the walkway to dry land.

At the end of the jetty, she let go his hand, and he even managed a smile at her. "Thanks for not pushing me in," he said. He was still shaking. "I wouldn't have blamed you if you had."

Maggie smiled ruefully at him. "We've made a mess of things, haven't we, Joe? Not just letting our marriage slip. The way we raised the children. I was trying to say sorry to Lucy yesterday - I'm just thankful she's come out of it OK in the end."

"Yeah, she's done herself proud," Joe nodded.

"And Thomas has turned out amazingly normal, considering," Maggie went on.

"Yup. He's a great lad."

They both looked at eachother, subdued. Then, on the pathway, they parted, Joe heading off to the camping pod, and Maggie back to the lodge.

*

Bel and Fox sat in the darkness, watching the

matinee. It was the last day the circus would be there, before the Big Top was taken down and they moved on. But though the circus could not stay, its influence would remain, for it had touched many lives with magic.

Bel had felt a great sense of importance about this occasion, and had dressed carefully, selecting her best outfit, a teal-coloured tunic dress, worn over spotty teal-coloured tights and a matching lace-trimmed underskirt - the colours set off her short dark hair perfectly. As she watched the show for a second time, Bel was just as mesmerised as she had been the first; in fact they seemed to have switched things up a bit today. Maybe they were trialling something new. Sophy was suspended from a white silk rope, huge puffy bunches of flowers suspended around her like pink clouds. The big top was a floral bower, pierced by rods of light, and flower-shaped clusters, all touched with a rose-gold glow. The silken rope gradually unravelled from her body as Sophy twisted and dropped downwards, revealing her bodysuit covered in diamonds.

Later, holding onto trapeze with one hand each, Sophy and a man embraced, illuminated by scarlet spotlights. Their bodies were strong, muscular. They complemented eachother perfectly. There was something intimate in their embrace. Was it just good acting, part of the show, Bel wondered, her gaze focusing sharply? Or could this man be Sophy's partner in life as well as the circus?

In the interval, Bel bought Fox an ice-cream. It was in a pink paper cup, and had strawberries, marshmallows and rainbow sprinkles. "Do you miss being in the show?" Bel asked her granddaughter as they settled back into their seats. Lucy had told her about the dancing that Fox had done in the show on the first night. Looking a bit sad, Fox nodded. Bel ruffled her curly hair affectionately. "But our holiday will be over in a couple of days," she told her. "You'll be back with your Mummy soon." The prospect pierced Bel through with sadness. She knew she would miss Fox terribly. She'd been kind of hoping that Fox might somehow end up staying with her forever, but she could see now that that had never been on the cards. The lights dimmed, the audience hushed and the show began again.

Acts came and went. And suddenly, there was Sophy again, spinning through a hoop, in a white dress and white stockings, swinging round and round through the hoop till she dropped suddenly, dramatically to cling on by her legs. The audience gasped. Bel was spellbound. Her daughter was magical; she was amazing - how had *she* ever produced such a creature? Sophy hung upside down, flame coloured hair fanning out. Triangles of magenta and white light cut across a royal blue background. All the while, outside the big top the sky was blue and the sun blazed. But inside, reality was suspended. High up in the roof of the big top it was black as night, illuminated by hundreds of little white starry lights.

Magic prevailed.

"I liked the bit where you and that chap were twined together –" Bel told Sophy afterwards. They were standing rather awkwardly in the caravan, struggling for something to say. Fox had popped off to use the bathroom.

"Oh, that's Raf," Sophy said, relieved to have something unproblematic to talk about.

"Raf?" Bel queried.

"Yes. He's my boyfriend. I love him, Mum."

There was an air of defensiveness in her tone, lest her mother should criticise the fact that he, too, was a circus performer, but Bel burst out, perhaps a little too eagerly, "Oh, that's fantastic, Sophy! Oh, how lovely."

Sophy was a little bemused. Since when had her mother been that starry-eyed about romance? "Well thanks, er – Mum."

Bel knew she must say her piece quickly; she didn't have much time before Fox came back from the bathroom. She took her daughter's hands and gazed earnestly into her eyes. Sophy for her part was too taken aback to pull away. "Sophy – darling," Bel began solemnly. "I just want to say again how very sorry I am for the way I've treated you in the past. Spending time with Fox these last few days has made me see how very wrong I was. I didn't approve of you living in the circus, though now I've seen you perform I can see of course that you're made for it. I was judging you by my own standards, because – well the truth is, I was scared of anything outside my own little world – you know, education, the nine to five. All these years I've been a big fish in a small pond. Inside my world, I feel in control. Outside of it, I feel scared." She gulped. "God, I feel terrible now, that you've been bringing up a child alone, when I should've been supporting you."

"It's OK, Mum, really –" Sophy felt overwhelmed by this sudden outpouring of emotion. It was too much to deal with after all this time, and she wanted to try to make it stop.

"No, listen, darling - to make it up to you, I want to give you some money. £10,000."

Sophy gasped. "That's too much. I couldn't accept that kind of money from you –"

"Why not?" Bel asked. "I've got more than enough for myself, and no-one else to spend it on. You can get something nice, for your caravan perhaps, or for Fox, or whatever you choose. Oh, God, what a pair we've been, me and your father…"

"Maybe Fox can stay with you sometimes, during the school holidays," Sophy offered, as an olive branch. It was the best she could come up with. She had considered the idea of Fox living half the time with her at the circus, and half the time with Bel or other relatives, but had ended up dismissing it. These last few days had made her realise just how much she missed her daughter, and she didn't really want to be apart from her ever again.

Bel nodded, and smiled. "That would be lovely." Secretly, though, she was wondering how practical that would actually be, with Sophy travelling all over the country, even popping over to Europe from time to time. How would an eight year old be able to travel all the way to Hampshire to spend time with her grandmother? Bel knew she would probably end up seeing Fox hardly at all. Then she had a sudden, wild thought - perhaps she could give up her job, and follow the circus! It was an exciting prospect, one that set her heart racing - however, whether she would actually do that in reality, remained to be seen.

*

Evening was approaching. Barty had popped over to the clubhouse for a drink. Everyone else was still out. Bored and restless, Lucy and Seb had been circling eachother all day, with Barty hovering in the background, both of them coming together for a bit, then drifting off to do their own thing for a while. It was as if they were all engaged in some bizarre mating ritual, Lucy thought. Seb was still taking every covert opportunity to persuade her to go away with him to Staffordshire. Even now, while Lucy was currently washing up the mugs from their coffee and Seb was leaning against the wall, watching her.

"You need to join the protest. You can't just sit back and trust the establishment to do the right thing!" It seemed he could talk like that endlessly. Lucy ran the soapy cloth round the insides of the mugs, enjoying the feel of the warm water on her skin. "The whole thing's imbalanced," he went on. "Power lies exclusively in the hands of the privileged elite, most of whom went to private school."

"Like you," she pointed out, enjoying their bantering.

"Yes, but that's not *my* fault." Seb scooped out some soap bubbles from the sink, and dabbed a blob on the end of her nose. "I wouldn't have *chosen* to go to private school." Lucy shrugged, then pulled the plug out of the sink, wiped her hands on the tea towel and walked off.

Seb followed her into the bedroom she shared with Barty, leaving the door ajar. Once inside, he slipped his arms round her waist. Lucy knew it was wrong, but she shivered with pleasure, and felt perversely thrilled at the thought that they could be discovered. Seb edged her up against the wall. "Seb!" she protested feebly. "Barty could come back at any minute."

"Do you want me to stop?"

In reply, Lucy pressed her hand to the back of his head, guiding his mouth towards hers. She knew she was behaving terribly, but she couldn't help herself.

"I love you, I love you," Sebastian said. "And I'm leaving tomorrow to go to Staffordshire. Come away with me."

Lucy gazed back at him, almost drowning in his eyes. She was nearly - so nearly - drawn in. But at the last moment she came to her senses. This was wrong. You shouldn't lay yourself open to magic and joy if it meant hurting someone. A person should always behave respectfully in regard of other people's feelings. She broke away from him. "No, Seb," she said quietly.

He gazed at her, stunned. "No to what?"

"I'm sorry, I can't come away with you. I need to stay with Barty. He needs me. He's got a shoot with *Hello* magazine coming up and he wants me there for that."

Seb gave a groan of frustration. "Sod the magazine article! He doesn't really need you. He's just using you! He wants you as an ornament to his political campaign. He doesn't really care about you as a *person*, Lucy!"

Lucy frowned. "But Florence told me to beware of *you*, Seb."

"Really?" He looked a bit offended. "Well Florence can be a bit of a gloom-monger, I suppose. I shouldn't take too much notice."

Lucy sighed, and shook her head. "Why are people always warning me about things? No-one seems to think I'm able to make my own decisions."

"That's not the point, Luce. The point is that you and I are meant to be together. I never felt about Florence the way I feel about you!" He drew her close again; his eyes were full of emotion and she could feel the beat of his heart against her chest. Seb lowered his head to kiss her again. Lucy felt herself melting, her resistance and resolve crumbling away.

At that moment, the bedroom door opened wider and Fox walked in, back from the circus. She was wearing a bluey-lilac swirly dress, covered in sparkles. The embracing couple turned to look at her, shocked. Fox looked straight at Seb, fixing him with her strange, beautiful gaze, one blue eye, one brown. It was uncertain as to what had made her come into the room at that moment. "You need to go, Sebastian," the little girl told him. "Out of this room. Now."

Shocked, Seb pulled away from Lucy, gave her one more hurt, questioning look, and then turned and walked from the room. Then Fox fixed Lucy with a stern gaze, before turning and sweeping out of the room herself. Left on her own, Lucy was dazed for a moment, then sank onto the bed and began to cry.

CHAPTER 11

The following morning dawned bright and sunny once again. The forecast kept predicting a break in the weather, but so far it had not happened. Everyone was gathered on the balcony finishing their breakfast, when Seb came through with his rucksack over his shoulder, and announced that he was leaving. Lucy dropped her piece of toast, the colour draining from her face.

"Well, I'll be sorry to see you go, son," Barty said heartily, scraping back his chair and getting up. There was a general murmuring of expressions of regret from the group. "I'll give you a lift to the station," Barty added.

"No thanks, Dad, I'd rather walk if it's all the same to you."

"OK, whatever, that's cool," Barty said.

Thomas drained the last of his orange juice. "So, where are you off to next, Seb, mate?"

"Staffordshire," Sebastian replied. "The woodlands are under threat from the rail link, and we have more tunnels to build." His eyes met Lucy's for a second, and a look of great intensity passed between them. There was a mingling of questioning, and reproach.

Then Lucy dragged her gaze away.

Joe got to his feet, polishing his glasses on the lapel of his jacket. "Well, good on you, Seb, I say." What a principled young man Sebastian was, he thought. If only he, himself, could live by such standards! Joe was feeling pretty down on himself once again, having been brooding over how he'd treated everyone. He'd messaged Rachael, saying he missed her and would love to see her. He told her that he and Maggie had now formally agreed to divorce, but so far she hadn't replied.

They all trooped through to the front of the lodge to say their farewells and wave Sebastian off – Maggie, Joe, Thomas, Bel, Fox, Barty and Lucy. There was a moment in the confusion of the crowd where Seb reached across and squeezed Lucy's hand tightly. If Barty noticed, he said nothing. Lucy had tears in her eyes which she fought to keep from falling. Meanwhile Fox was watching Seb intently, as if to make sure he was definitely leaving – as if she was the moral guardian of the house. Seb *was* leaving; he was walking off. They all watched as his tall, dark-haired figure receded off up the track. At one point near the bend in the road, he turned around and gave one final wave.

Seb had gone. His ego was bruised but no doubt he would recover. Lucy, however, felt a hole where her heart should be, and was perilously close to crying. She knew that at some point in the future their paths would cross again, but that it must only ever be as friends. It was hard to take. The pain she was feeling made her ask herself some questions - it was true that she loved Barty, but did she love him *enough?* And to make matters worse, for Barty and herself at least, the holiday was over. They were leaving later that day, so as to be back in time for the magazine shoot.

Mere moments after Sebastian disappeared from sight, there was an ominous rumble from the heavens. Fox clung to her grandmother in fear. "Thunder!" Maggie exclaimed, stating the obvious. There was another rumble, then the sky darkened and it began to rain.

"Quick, let's get inside, before we get soaked," Bel told Fox, scooping her up in her arms. Everyone followed them, hurrying for the shelter of the lodge. "I'm going back to the pod," Thomas called. "See ya later."

"Oh dear, poor Seb will get wet," Lucy murmured to Barty, who had taken her hand and was leading her gently inside.

"He'll be fine," Barty replied confidently. "He's used to braving the elements."

Everyone gave a wide berth to the tub of bait that had been left by the steps to the lodge. The fishing hadn't proved too productive, and after a few early attempts Joe and Barty had abandoned it. Like house guests that have outstayed their welcome, the bait was starting to stink. "We'll have to dispose of that soon," Joe remarked to Barty as he walked past it. "Or it'll stink the place out and we'll lose our deposit."

But Barty had bigger things on his mind than the stinking bait. Without letting go of Lucy's hand, he drew her purposefully into the bedroom.

Lucy felt a twinge of fear, wondering if he had discovered her affair with Seb, and was about to confront her over it. "It's been quite an, er, eventful few days," Barty began as they stood facing eachother, and Lucy's anxiety intensified. However, she was extremely surprised when he continued, "And it's, er, made me realise how much you mean to me and, er, how devastated I'd be if I lost you old girl so..." There was a brief pause while thunder once again rumbled overhead. "...I was wondering, darling, whether you'd consider being my wife?"

Lucy widened her eyes. "Is that a proposal?" she asked in shock.

Barty assumed – wrongly - that she was accusing him of not being romantic enough. With an effort he got down on one knee. He took a gold signet ring off his little finger, and slid it onto the fourth finger of her left hand. "There. Will that do for now, til I can get you something better?"

"Oh Barty," Lucy said. She had thought she would be ecstatically happy at this moment, a moment she'd waited for for so long, but instead she felt a strange pain tug at her heartstrings. "You're very sweet but I don't know ..." Gently she took the ring off and slid it back onto his finger. "Can I have some time to think about it?"

*

Once they were all cooped up inside the lodge, Fox began to get restless. Barty and Lucy had disappeared off to their bedroom, while Maggie had popped to the loo. The remaining three drifted back through to the balcony, to the remains of the hastily abandoned breakfast. Joe and Bel stayed under the part of the balcony that was sheltered by the porch. Fox began turning cartwheels on the balcony. She was wearing the yellow sundress again, and it turned and swirled like the petals of a flower. Then suddenly she got up on the edge of the balcony and began balancing along it, arms out, as if she was on a gymnast's beam.

"Fox, no!" Bel shouted. "Get down from there at once!"

The wood was slippery from rain. Before anyone knew what was happening, Fox had slipped off the balcony and fallen into the lake with a scream.

"Oh God oh God," Bel shrieked. "I don't think she can swim!"

Joe watched in horror. The water was dark, terrifying. Who knew what was down there? He continued to stare, frozen into inaction. He was a right cowardly piece of shit, he knew. Surely anything was better than feeling like this, even – Not allowing himself to think any more, he leapt to his feet, stripping off his jacket, throwing off his glasses, then vaulting over the edge of the balcony and into the lake with a huge splash. Joe hit the water; it filled his eyes and mouth, tasting of fish; algae. He bobbed to the surface. Revolted, he spat the water out, shook it from his hair. Now he was functioning on adrenaline; operating on instinct. He vaguely remembered doing lifesaving classes at school years ago. With an effort he swam up to where Fox was struggling, making sure to approach her from behind as the classes had taught. He managed to wrap his arm around her waist, gripping her tightly, and then began to manoeuvre her back to shore using a clumsy side-stroke.

Meanwhile, Maggie had clambered down the bank of the lake and had splashed down into the shallows. Joe was getting closer and closer to the water's edge. The rain continued to pour down.

"That's it, Joe, give her to me!" Maggie shouted. She waded the last couple of feet towards him and grabbed Fox from his arms. Fox's eyes were open; she was still conscious; it seemed she was safe. Maggie staggered up the bank, the little girl in her arms, the yellow sundress streaming water. When Maggie asked Fox if she was OK, she nodded and then began to cry. Bel rushed forward, taking her from Maggie, wrapping her in a towel. The two women hurried the child into the lodge. Exhausted, Joe felt himself drifting away from the shore once again, sinking lower into the water, so that just his head was above the surface. Well, who cared? Drowning might not be so bad. It would do everyone else a favour – after all, he'd been one heck of a nuisance to them all.

From nearby there was the sound of a car coming to a halt; a door slamming shut. And suddenly Rachael was there at the water's edge, standing there in the driving rain. Rachael! She was wearing her lovely orang-utan patterned dress and it was getting soaked! Seeing her, something in Joe rallied, and, despite his exhaustion, he renewed his efforts to swim to the shore. When he was nearly there, Rachael reached out a hand and dragged him out, his feet squelching into the mud. Some of the other holidaymakers had rushed to the scene, having heard the shrieks from the balcony. They included barbecue man, minus the novelty apron.

"Everything all right here, folks?" he asked, looking concerned.

"Yes, panic over," Rachael smiled back, a piece of pond weed dangling from her bright yellow fringe. "I think we'll be fine now. Thanks a lot, though."

"Rachael!" Joe spluttered, as the crowd dispersed. He still could not believe she was there, at the lodge. "What the –"

"Your son told me you were here," she said. "You idiotic man, I thought I'd lost you!"

"I love you, Rachael," he said, collapsing into her arms.

"I love you too," Rachael said. "But let's get you indoors, shall we, before you die of hypothermia."

Lucy came running out of the lodge. "Dad! Are

you OK? I hear you were the hero of the hour!" She stopped suddenly, staring at her father embracing an unfamiliar woman. "Oh! I'm not interrupting anything, am I?"

EPILOGUE

Twelve Weeks Later...

The letter-box clattered and, going through to the hall, Maggie saw that there was a postcard from Joe. He and his new woman Rachael were now living in a dilapidated shack in north Wales. Well, rather them than me! Maggie thought - she liked her mod cons - though they seemed to be happy. According to the postcard, Rachael was 'still doing her counselling' – well, Maggie hadn't even known she'd done it in the first place.

So there they were, Joe and Rachael, just the two of them, in their little love-nest. At one point it had looked like Thomas might join his dad, but then he'd unexpectedly been offered a job as a Data Scientist only a ten mile commute away from home, and had decided to stay put with Maggie - which she was secretly pleased about. Since then, Thomas had been revelling in his new, bigger paycheck and had been splurging a bit – new clothes, a birdwatching telescope, and luxury takeaway delivery at all hours of the day and night.

After briefly glancing over the postcard now, Maggie screwed it up and chucked it in the kitchen bin. No sooner had she done this than her phone rang. Now, where had she left the blasted thing? She padded through to the sitting-room, and saw from the caller display that it was Lucy. Maggie felt a twinge of pleasure mixed with anxiety. Shortly after the holiday, Lucy had left Barty, and had since got a job at a rival magazine. Lucy said she'd definitely done the right thing by splitting from her partner - and yet it seemed to Maggie whenever they spoke as though her daughter was nursing some private heartache. Maggie picked the phone up now. "Hello, darling," she said cautiously. "How are you?"

"Hi, Mum." To Maggie's relief she sounded fine and, uncharacteristically for Lucy, she seemed to be in a confiding mood. Lucy casually mentioned that she was feeling a bit nauseous and had missed a couple of periods, but then, as she told her mother, her periods had always been erratic, and so far she had postponed going to the doctor. Her tone seemed to forbid Maggie asking any further questions.

After a bit more chit-chat, Maggie told her daughter to take care of herself, and that she could call anytime. "Love you," she said to Lucy.

"Love you too."

"Bye." Then Maggie clicked off her phone and went to gaze out of the front window at the dusty street. They were now nearing the end of the school summer holidays. Soon it would be Autumn, which used to fill Maggie with a melancholy air. In recent years, though, she'd noticed that people had started to see autumn more as something positive, something to embrace. Maggie actually loved the seasonal stuff that they sold now. Wreaths and garlands of fake autumn leaves, orange, russet, beige. Pumpkin spice latte in takeaway cups from Starbucks, and similarly scented big orange candles in jars. Joe would not approve. He would say it was tacky, un-green, and that they found a way to monetise everything in the end. But sod Joe, Maggie thought. Thinking of her daughter, her son, and herself, Maggie felt life still had some very interesting things in store, just around the corner.

The End

Printed in Great Britain
by Amazon

17703894R00135